THE NEW WIN...

General Editors: Anne, and Ian Serraillier

200

One Day
in the Life of
Ivan Denisovich

This contemporary masterpiece, in the great Russian
tradition, gives an unforgettable picture of human life
in inhuman conditions

ALEXANDER SOLZHENITSYN

ONE DAY
IN THE
LIFE
OF
IVAN
DENISOVICH

TRANSLATED BY
RALPH PARKER

HEINEMANN EDUCATIONAL BOOKS
LONDON

Heinemann Educational Books Ltd
22 Bedford Square, London WC1B 3HH
LONDON EDINBURGH MELBOURNE AUCKLAND
HONG KONG SINGAPORE KUALA LUMPUR NEW DELHI
NAIROBI JOHANNESBURG IBADAN
EXETER (NH) KINGSTON PORT OF SPAIN

ISBN 0 435 12200 2
First published in the Soviet Union 1962
English translation © 1963, Victor Gollancz Ltd
First published 1963
First published in the New Windmill Series 1974
Reprinted 1976, 1978, 1981

TRANSLATOR'S DEDICATION

To my grandson, Dimitri Ivanovich,
with thoughts of the future

Printed and bound in Great Britain by
Butler & Tanner Ltd, Frome and London

ABOUT THE AUTHOR

ALEXANDER ISAYEVICH SOLZHENITSYN was born in Rostov-on-Don in 1918. His father was a white-collar worker, his mother a school teacher. It was his mother who brought him up and with whom he lived until, just after graduating at Rostov University as a mathematician—he took a correspondence course in literature simultaneously—he was called up to the Red Army. In 1942, at the age of twenty-four, he was promoted from the ranks to become the commander of an artillery battery. He served at the front without a break, being twice decorated and being promoted to the rank of captain, until February 1945, when he was arrested in a village in Russian-occupied East Prussia on the charge of having made remarks derogatory to Stalin. The next eight years Solzhenitsyn spent in various labour-camps, first in "general" camps in the Arctic where political prisoners were imprisoned with common criminals, then in Beria's "special" camps, organized for prisoners serving sentences, ranging from eight to twenty-five years, under the notorious Article 58 of a Criminal Code that has now been replaced. The camp in which Solzhenitsyn—and his hero Ivan Denisovich—served his term of imprisonment was in the region of Karaganda in northern Kazakhstan. In 1953, the year of Stalin's death, Solzhenitsyn was released, but it was not until he had spent three further years in exile that, shortly after the 20th Party Congress at which Khrushchev denounced Stalin in his secret speech, his case was reviewed, his sentence quashed "in the absence of corpus delicti" and he was able to join the hundreds of thousands of the "rehabilitated". He then settled in a village near the central Russian town of Ryazan, married a young teacher of chemistry, and began to teach physics and mathematics at a secondary school.

For the next three or four years he wrote continuously, and in late 1960 submitted his novel *One Day in the Life of Ivan Denisovich* and two short stories to the Russian poet Alexander Tvardovsky, who at that time was editing the literary journal *Novy Mir* (New World) for the Union of Soviet Writers. Tvardovsky, being a member of the Central Committee, was in a position to obtain authoritative opinions on *One Day*, quoting in its favour the words Khrushchev used at the 22nd Party Congress: " . . . it is our duty to make a painstaking and thorough analysis of these things connected with the abuse of power. Time passes, we are all mortal, but as long as we are working we can and must elucidate much and tell the truth to the Party and the people. . . . This we must do so that such things may never happen again."

The book was published in November 1962. The author paid one short visit to Moscow, shunned the press and returned to Ryazan; no longer teaching, but determined to remain undisturbed in the literary career he had planned for himself.

However, this was not to be. His fearless views about the abuse of power in his own country, coupled with his international acclaim as a writer (in 1974 his work was available in 79 languages), became an increasing embarrassment to the Soviet authorities. In February 1974 they accused him of "systematic activities incompatible with the holding of Soviet citizenship." Deprived of his citizenship, he left Russia and went to live in Zürich, where his wife and three children, his mother-in-law and stepson soon joined him.

As USUAL, AT five o'clock that morning reveille was sounded by the blows of a hammer on a length of rail hanging up near the staff quarters. The intermittent sounds barely penetrated the window-panes on which the frost lay two fingers thick, and they ended almost as soon as they'd begun. It was cold outside, and the camp-guard was reluctant to go on beating out the reveille for long.

The clanging ceased, but everything outside still looked like the middle of the night when Ivan Denisovich Shukhov got up to go to the bucket. It was pitch dark except for the yellow light cast on the window by three lamps—two in the outer zone, one inside the camp itself.

And no one came to unbolt the barrack-hut door; there was no sound of the barrack-orderlies pushing a pole into place to lift the barrel of nightsoil and carry it out.

Shukhov never overslept reveille. He always got up at once, for the next ninety minutes, until they assembled for work, belonged to him, not to the authorities, and any old-timer could always earn a bit—by sewing a pair of over-mittens for someone out of old sleeve lining; or bringing some rich lag in the team his dry valenki[1]—right up to his bunk, so that he wouldn't have to stumble barefoot round the heap of boots looking for his own pair; or going the rounds of the store-huts, offering to be of service, sweeping up this or fetching that; or going to the mess-hall to collect bowls from the tables and bring them stacked to the dishwashers—you're sure to be given something to eat there, though there were plenty of others at that game, more than plenty—and, what's worse, if you found a bowl with something left in it you could hardly resist licking it out. But Shukhov had never forgotten the words of his first team-leader, Kuziomin—a hard-bitten prisoner who had already been in for twelve years by 1943—who told the newcomers, just in from the front, as they sat beside a fire in a desolate cutting in the forest:

"Here, lads, we live by the law of the taiga. But even here

[1] Knee-length boots for winter wear.

3

people manage to live. D'you know who are the ones the camps finish off? Those who lick other men's left-overs, those who set store by the doctors, and those who peach on their mates."

As for peachers, he was wrong there. Those people were sure to get through camp all right. Only, they were saving their own skin at the expense of other people's blood.

Shukhov always arose at reveille. But this day he didn't. He had felt queer the evening before, feverish, with pains all over his body. He hadn't been able to get warm all through the night. Even in his sleep he had felt at one moment that he was getting seriously ill, at another that he was getting better. He had longed for the morning not to come.

But the morning came as usual.

Anyway, it wasn't surprising that he'd felt cold in the night. That ice on the window-panes! And the white cob-webs of hoar-frost all along the huge hut where the walls joined the ceiling!

He didn't get up. He lay there in his bunk on the top tier, his head buried in a blanket and a coat, his two feet stuffed into one sleeve, with the end tucked under, of his wadded jacket. He couldn't see, but his ears told him everything going on in the barrack-room and especially in the corner his team occupied. He heard the heavy tread of the orderlies carrying one of the big barrels of nightsoil along the passage outside. A light job, that was considered, a job for the infirm, but just you try and carry out the muck without spilling any. He heard some of the 75th slamming bunches of boots on to the floor from the drying-shed. Now their own lads were doing it (it was their own team's turn, too, to dry valenki). Tiurin, the team-leader, and his deputy Pavlo put on their valenki without a word but he heard their bunks creaking. Now Pavlo would be going off to the bread-stores and Tiurin to the staff quarters to see the P.P.D.[1]

Ah, but not simply to report as usual to the authorities who distributed the daily assignments. Shukhov remembered that this morning his fate hung in the balance: they wanted to shift the 104th from the building-shops to a new site, the "Socialist Way of Life" settlement. It lay in open country covered with snow-drifts, and before anything else could be done there they would have to dig pits and put up posts and attach barbed wire to them.

[1] Production Planning Department.

4

Wire themselves in, s⎼⎼⎼ ⎼⎼⎼⎼⎼⎼ ⎼n't run away. Only then would they start building.

There wouldn't be a warm corner for a whole month. Not a dog-kennel. And fires were out of the question. Where was the firewood to come from? Warm up with the work, that was your only salvation.

No wonder the team-leader looked so worried, that was his responsibility—to elbow some other team, some bunch of clod-hoppers, into the assignment instead of the 104th. Of course he wouldn't get the authorities to agree if he turned up empty-handed. He'd have to take a pound of pork-fat to the senior official there, if not a couple of pounds.

There's never any harm in trying, so why not have a go at the sick-bay and get a few days off if you can? After all, he did feel as though every limb was out of joint.

Then Shukhov wondered which of the camp-guards was on duty that morning. It was "One-and-a-half" Ivan's turn, he recalled. Ivan was a thin, weedy, dark-eyed sergeant. At first sight he looked a real terror, but when you got to know him he turned out to be the most good-natured of the guards on duty: he didn't put you in the lock-up, he didn't haul you off before the authorities. So Shukhov decided he could lie in his bunk a little longer, at least while Hut 9 was at the mess-hall.

The whole four-bunk frame began to shake and sway. Two of its occupants were getting up simultaneously: Shukhov's top-tier neighbour, Alyosha the Baptist, and Buinovsky, the ex-naval captain down below.

The orderlies, after removing both the barrels of night-soil, began to quarrel about which of them should go for hot water. They quarrelled naggingly, like old women.

"Hey you, spluttering like a couple of squibs!" bellowed the electric welder in the 20th team. "Make it up." He flung a boot at them.

The boot thudded against a post. The squabbling stopped.

In the adjacent team the deputy team-leader growled quietly: "Vasily Fyodorovich, they've cheated us again at the supply-hatch, the slimy rats: they should have given us four nine-hundred gram loaves and I've only got three. Who's to go short?"

He kept his voice down, but of course everyone in the team

heard him and waited fearfully to learn who would be losing a slice of bread that evening.

Shukhov went on lying on his sawdust mattress, as hard as a board from long wear. If only it could be one thing or the other: let him fall into a real fever or let his aching joints ease up.

Meanwhile Alyosha was murmuring his prayers and Buinovsky had returned from the latrines, announcing to no one in particular but with a sort of malicious glee:

"Well, sailors, grit your teeth. It's thirty below, for sure."

Shukhov decided to report sick.

At that very moment his blanket and jacket were imperiously jerked off him. He flung his coat away from his face and sat up. Looking up at him, his head level with the top bunk, was the lean figure of The Tartar.

So the fellow was on duty out of turn and had stolen up.

"S 854", The Tartar read from the white strip that had been stitched to the back of his black jacket. "Three days' penalty with work."

The moment they heard that peculiar choking voice of his, everyone who wasn't up yet in the whole dimly-lit hut, where two hundred men slept in bug-ridden bunks, stirred to life and began hurriedly dressing.

"What for, citizen[1] chief?" asked Shukhov with more chagrin than he felt in his voice.

With work—that wasn't half so bad. They gave you hot food and you had no time to start thinking. Real lock-up was when you were kept back from work.

"Failing to get up at reveille. Follow me to the camp commandant's office," said The Tartar lazily.

His crumpled, hairless face was imperturbable. He turned, looking round for another victim, but now everybody, in dim corners and under the lights, in upper bunks and lower, had thrust their legs into their black wadded trousers, or, already dressed, had wrapped their coats round them and hurried to the door to get out of the way until The Tartar had left.

Had Shukhov been punished for something he deserved he wouldn't have felt so resentful. What hurt him was that he was always one of the first to be up. But he knew he couldn't plead

[1] Prisoners were not allowed to use the word comrade.

6

with The Tartar. And, protesting merely for the sake of form, he hitched up his trousers (a bedraggled scrap of cloth had been sewn on them, just above the left knee, with a faded black number), slipped on his jacket (here the same digits appeared twice—on the chest and on the back), fished his valenki from the heap on the floor, put his hat on (with his number on a patch of cloth at the front), and followed The Tartar out of the barrack-room.

The whole 104th saw him go, but no one said a word: what was the use, and anyway what could they say ? The team-leader might have tried something, but he wasn't there. And Shukhov said nothing to anyone. He didn't want to irritate The Tartar. Anyway he could rely on his mates to keep his breakfast for him.

The two men left the hut. The cold made Shukhov gasp.

Two powerful searchlights swept the camp from the farthest watch-towers. The border-lights, as well as those inside the camp, were on. There were so many of them that they outshone the stars.

With the snow creaking under their boots, the prisoners hurried away, each on his own business, some to the parcels office, some to hand in cereals to be cooked in the "individual" kitchen. All kept their heads down, buried in their buttoned-up coats, and all were chilled to the bone, not so much from the actual cold as from the prospect of having to spend the whole day in it. But The Tartar in his old army coat with the greasy blue tabs walked at a steady pace, as though the cold meant nothing to him.

They walked past the high wooden fence round the lock-up, the only brick building in the camp; past the barbed wire that protected the camp bakery from the prisoners; past the corner of the staff quarters where the length of frosted rail hung on thick strands of wire; past another pole with a thermometer hanging to it (in a sheltered spot, so that the registered temperature shouldn't drop too low). Shukhov looked hopefully out of the corner of an eye at the milk-white tube: if it had shown −41° they ought not to be sent out to work. But today it was nowhere near −41°.

They walked into the staff quarters and The Tartar led him straight through to the guard-room; and Shukhov realized, as he had guessed on the way there, that he wasn't being sent to the lock-up at all—it was simply that the guard-room floor needed scrubbing. The Tartar told him he was going to let him off, and ordered him to scrub.

Scrubbing the guard-room floor had been the job of a special prisoner who wasn't sent to work outside the camp—a staff orderly. The fellow had long ago made himself at home in the staff quarters; he had access to the offices of the camp commandant, the man in charge of discipline, and the security officer (the Father Confessor, they called him). When working for them he sometimes heard things that even the guards didn't know, and after a time he got uppish, and came to consider scrubbing the floor for rank-and-file camp-guards a bit beneath him. Having sent for him once or twice the guards discovered what was in the wind, and began to pick on other prisoners for the floor-scrubbing.

In the guard-room the stove was throwing out a fierce heat. Two guards in grubby tunics were playing draughts, and a third, who had not bothered to remove his sheepskin and valenki, lay snoring on a narrow bench. In one corner of the room stood an empty pail with a rag inside.

Shukhov was delighted. He thanked The Tartar for letting him off and said: "From now on I'll never get up late again."

The rule in this place was a simple one: when you'd finished you left. And now that he'd been given work to do, Shukhov's aches and pains seemed to have gone. He picked up the pail and, bare-handed—in his hurry he'd forgotten to take his mittens from under his pillow—went to the well.

Several of the team-leaders who were on their way to the P.P.D. had gathered near the pole with the thermometer, and one of the younger ones, a former Hero of the Soviet Union, shinned up it and wiped the instrument.

The others shouted advice from below:

"See you don't breathe on it. It'll put up the temperature."

"Put it up ? Not —— likely. *My* breath won't have any effect."

Tiurin of the 104th—Shukhov's team—was not among them. Shukhov put down the pail, tucked his hands into his sleeves and watched with interest.

The man up the pole shouted hoarsely:

"Twenty-seven and a half. Not a bloody bit more."

And, taking another look to be sure, slid down.

"Oh, it's cock-eyed. It always lies," someone said. "D'you think they'd ever hang one up that gave the true temperature?"

The team-leaders scattered. Shukhov ran to the well. The frost was trying to nip his ears under his ear-flaps, which he had lowered but not tied.

The top of the well was so thickly coated with ice that he only just managed to slip the bucket into the hole. The rope hung stiff as a ramrod.

With numb hands he carried the streaming bucket back to the guard-room and plunged his hands into the water. It felt warm.

The Tartar was no longer there. The guards—there were four now—stood in a group. They'd given up their draughts and their kip and were arguing about how much millet they were going to get in January (food was in short supply at the settlement, and although rationing had long since come to an end certain articles were sold to them, at a discount, which were not available to the civilian inhabitants).

"Shut that door, you scum. There's a draught," said one of the guards.

No sense in getting your boots wet in the morning. Even if Shukhov had dashed back to his hut he wouldn't have found another pair to change into. During eight years' imprisonment he had known various systems for allocating footwear: there'd been times when he'd gone through the winter without valenki at all, or leather boots either, and had had to make shift with bast sandals or a sort of galoshes made of scraps of motor tyres— "Chetezes" they called them, after the Cheliabinsk tractor works. Now the footwear situation seemed better; in October Shukhov had received (thanks to Pavlo, whom he trailed to the store) a pair of ordinary, hard-wearing leather boots, big enough for a double thickness of foot-cloth. For a week he went about as though he'd been given a birthday present, kicking his new heels. Then in December the valenki arrived, and, oh, wasn't life wonderful?

But some devil in the book-keeper's office had whispered in the commandant's ear that valenki should be issued only to those who surrendered their boots. It was against the rules for a prisoner to possess two pairs of footwear at the same time. So Shukhov had to choose. Either he'd have to wear leather throughout the winter, or surrender the boots and wear valenki even in the thaw. He'd taken such good care of his new boots, softening the leather with grease! Ah, nothing had been so hard to part with in all his eight years in camps as that pair of boots! They were tossed into a common heap. Not a hope of finding your own pair in the spring.

Now Shukhov knew what he had to do. He dexterously pulled his feet out of the valenki, put the valenki in a corner, stuffed his foot-cloths into them (his spoon tinkled on the floor—though he'd made himself ready for the lock-up in haste he hadn't forgotten his spoon), and, bare-foot, sploshed the water right under the guard's valenki.

"Hey there, skunk, take it easy," one of the guards shouted, putting his feet on a chair.

"Rice?" another went on. "Rice is in a different category. You can't compare millet with rice."

"How much water are you going to use, idiot? Who on earth washes like that?"

"I'll never get it clean otherwise, citizen chief. It's thick with muck."

"Didn't you ever watch your woman scrubbing the floor, pig?"

Shukhov drew himself up, the streaming rag in his hand. He smiled ingenuously, revealing the gaps in his teeth, the result of a touch of scurvy at Ust-Izhma in 1943. And what a touch it was— his exhausted stomach wouldn't hold any kind of food, and his bowels could move nothing but a bloody flux. But now only a lisp remained from that old trouble.

"I was taken away from my woman in 'forty-one, citizen chief. I've forgotten what she was like."

"That's the way the scum wash. . . . They don't know how to do a —— thing and don't want to learn. They're not worth the bread we give them. We ought to feed them on shit."

"Anyway, what's the —— sense in washing it every day? Who can stand the damp? Look here, you, 854. Just wipe it over lightly to make it moist and then —— off."

"No, you can't compare millet with rice."

Shukhov knew how to manage anything.

Work was like a stick. It had two ends. When you worked for the knowing you gave them quality; when you worked for a fool you simply gave him eye-wash.

Otherwise, everybody would have croaked long ago. They all knew that.

Shukhov wiped the floor-boards with a damp rag so that no dry patches remained, tossed the rag behind the stove without wringing it out, pulled on his valenki near the door, threw out the rest of the water on to the path used by the camp authorities, and, cutting off corners, made a dash past the bath-house and the dark, cold club to the mess-hall.

He still had to fit in a visit to the sick-bay. He was again all aches and pains. And there was that guard outside the mess-hall to be dodged: the camp commandant had issued strict orders that prisoners on their own were to be picked up and thrown into the lock-up.

That morning—a stroke of luck—there was no crowd, no queues, outside the mess. Walk in.

The air was as thick as in a bath-house. An icy wave blew in through the door and met the steam rising from the skilly. The teams sat at tables or crowded the aisles in between, waiting for places to be freed. Shouting to each other through the crush, two or three men from each team carried bowls of skilly and porridge on wooden trays and tried to find room for them on the tables. Look at that bloody stiff-backed fool. He doesn't hear, he's jolted a tray. Splash, splash! You've a hand free, swipe him on the back of the neck. That's the way. Don't stand there blocking the aisle, looking for something to filch!

There at the table, before dipping his spoon in, a young man crossed himself. A West Ukrainian, that meant, and a new arrival too.

As for the Russians, they'd forgotten which hand to cross themselves with.

They sat in the cold mess-hall, most of them eating with their hats on, eating slowly, picking out putrid little fish from under leaves of boiled black cabbage and spitting the bones out on the table. When the bones formed a heap and it was the turn of another team, someone would sweep them off and they'd be trodden into a mush on the floor. But it was considered bad manners to spit the fishbones straight out on the floor.

Two rows of supports ran down the middle of the hall and near one of them sat Fetiukov of the 104th. It was he who was keeping

Shukhov's breakfast for him. Fetiukov had the last place in his team, lower than Shukhov's. From the outside, everyone in the team looked the same—their numbered black coats were identical —but within the team there were great distinctions. Everyone had his grade. Buinovsky, for instance, was not the sort to sit keeping another zek's[1] bowl for him. And Shukhov wouldn't take on any old job either. There were others lower than him.

Fetiukov caught sight of Shukhov and with a sigh surrendered his place.

"It's all cold. I was just going to eat your helping. Thought you were in the lock-up."

He didn't hang around: no hope for any left-overs to scrape off from Shukhov's skilly.

Shukhov pulled his spoon out of his boot. His little treasure. It had been with him his whole time in the North, he'd cast it with his own hands in sand out of aluminium wire and it was embossed with the words "Ust-Izhma 1944."

Then he removed his hat from his clean-shaven head—however cold it might be, he could never bring himself to eat with his hat on— and stirred the cold skilly, taking a quick look to see what kind of helping they'd given him. An average one. They hadn't ladled it from the top of the cauldron, but they hadn't ladled it from the bottom either. Fetiukov was the sort who when he was looking after someone else's bowl took the potatoes from it.

The only good thing about skilly was that it was hot, but Shukhov's portion had grown quite cold. However, he ate it with his usual slow concentration. No need to hurry, not even for a house on fire. Sleep apart, the only time a prisoner lives for himself is ten minutes in the morning at breakfast, five minutes over dinner and five at supper.

The skilly was the same every day. Its composition depended on the kind of vegetable provided that winter. Nothing but salted carrots last year, which meant that from September to June the skilly was plain carrot. This year it was black cabbage. The most nourishing time of the year was June: then all vegetables came to an end and were replaced by groats. The worse time was July: then they shredded nettles into the pot.

The little fish were more bone than flesh; the flesh had been

[1] Abbreviation of Russian prisoner.

12

boiled off the bone and had disintegrated, leaving a few remnants on head and tail. Without neglecting a single fish-scale or particle of flesh on the brittle skeleton, Shukhov went on champing his teeth and sucking the bones, spitting the remains on the table. He ate everything—the gills, the tail, the eyes when they were still in their sockets but not when they'd been boiled out and floated in the bowl separately—great fish-eyes! Not then. The others laughed at him for that.

This morning Shukhov economised. As he hadn't returned to the hut he hadn't drawn his rations, so he ate his breakfast without bread. He'd eat the bread later. Might be even better that way.

After the skilly there was magara porridge. It had grown cold too, and had set into a solid lump. Shukhov broke it up into pieces. It wasn't only that the porridge was cold—it was tasteless when hot, and left you no sense of having filled your belly. Just grass, except that it was yellow, and looked like millet. They'd got the idea of serving it instead of cereals from the Chinese, it was said. When boiled, a bowlful of it weighed nearly a pound. Not much of a porridge but that was what it passed for.

Licking his spoon and tucking it back into his boot, Shukhov put on his hat and went to the sick-bay.

The sky was still quite dark. The camp lights drove away the stars. The broad beams of the two searchlights were still sweeping the zone. When this camp, this "special" camp, had been organized, the security forces had a lot of flares left over from the war, and whenever there was a power failure they shot up flares over the zone—white, green and red—just like real war. Later they stopped using them. To save money, maybe.

It seemed just as dark as at reveille but the experienced eye could easily distinguish, by various small signs, that soon the order to go to work would be given. Khromoi's assistant (Khromoi, the mess orderly, had an assistant whom he fed) went off to summon number 6 Hut to breakfast. This was the building occupied by the infirm, who did not leave the zone. An old, bearded artist shuffled off to the C.E.D.[1] for the brush and paint he needed to touch up the numbers on the prisoners' uniforms. The Tartar was there again, cutting across the mustering-ground with long, rapid strides in the direction of the staff quarters. In

[1] Culture and Education Department.

general there were fewer people about, which meant that everyone had gone off to some corner or other to warm up during those last precious minutes.

Shukhov was canny enough to hide from The Tartar round a corner of the barracks: the fellow would stick to him if he nabbed him again. Anyway, you should never be conspicuous. The main thing was never to be seen by a camp-guard on your own, only in a group. Who was to know the fellow wasn't looking for someone to saddle with a job, or wouldn't pounce on a man just for spite? Hadn't they been round the barracks and read them that new regulation? You had to take off your hat to a guard five paces before passing him, and replace it two paces after. There were guards who slopped past as if blind, not caring a damn, but for others the new rule was a godsend. How many prisoners had been flung in the lock-up because of that hat business? Oh no, better to stand round the corner.

The Tartar passed by, and now Shukhov finally decided for the sick-bay. But suddenly he remembered that the tall Lett in Hut 7 had told him to come and buy a couple of glasses of home-grown tobacco that morning before they went to work, something Shukhov had clean forgotten in all the excitement. The Lett had received a parcel the previous evening, and who knew but that tomorrow none of the tobacco would be left, and then he'd have to wait a month for another parcel? The Lett's tobacco was good stuff, strong and fragrant, greyish-brown.

Shukhov kicked his heels in vexation. Should he turn back and go to the Lett? But it was such a short distance to the sick-bay and he jogged on. The snow creaked audibly underfoot as he approached the door.

Inside, the corridor was, as usual, so clean that he felt quite scared to step on the floor. And the walls were painted with white enamel. And all the furniture was white.

The surgery doors were all shut. The doctor must still be in bed. The man on duty was a medical assistant—a young man called Kolya Vdovushkin. He was seated at a clean little table, wearing a small white cap and a snow-white smock. Writing something.

There was no one else in sight.

Shukhov took off his hat as if in the presence of one of the authorities and, letting his eyes slide, in the camp manner, where

14

they had no business to, he noticed that Kolya was writing in even, neatly-spaced lines and that each line, starting a little way from the edge of the page, began with a capital letter. He realized at once, of course, that Kolya was not doing official work but something on the side. But that was none of his business.

"Well, Nikolai Semyonich, it's like this . . . I'm feeling sort of . . . unwell . . . ," said Shukhov shamefacedly, as if coveting something that didn't belong to him.

Kolya Vdovushkin raised his big placid eyes from his work. His number was covered up by his smock.

"Why've you come so late? Why didn't you report sick last night? You know very well there are no consulting hours in the morning. The sick-list has already been sent to the planning department."

Shukhov knew all this. He knew too that it was no simple matter to get on the sick-list in the evening.

"But after all, Kolya. . . . You see, when I should have come . . . last night . . . it didn't ache."

"And now it does? And what is it?"

"Well, if you stop to think of it, nothing aches, but I feel ill all over."

Shukhov was not one of those who hung about the sick-bay. Vdovushkin knew this. But in the morning he had the right to exempt from work two men only, and he'd already exempted them: their names were written down under the glass—it was greenish—on his desk, and he'd drawn a line across the page.

"Well, you ought to have considered that earlier. What are you thinking about? Reporting sick just before the muster. Come on, take this."

He pulled a thermometer out of one of the jars where they stood in holes cut in pieces of gauze, wiped it dry and handed it to Shukhov, who put it in his armpit.

Shukhov sat on a bench near the wall, right at the very end, so that he nearly tipped it up. He sat in that uncomfortable way, involuntarily emphasizing that he was unfamiliar with the place and that he'd come there on some minor matter.

Vdovushkin went on writing.

The sick-bay lay in the most remote and deserted corner of the zone, where no sounds of any sort reached it. No clocks or watches ticked there—prisoners were not allowed to carry watches, the authorities knew the time for them. Even mice didn't scratch there; they'd all been dealt with by the hospital cat, placed there for the purpose.

For Shukhov it was a strange experience to sit in that spick-and-span room, in such quietness, to sit under the bright lamps for five long minutes doing nothing. He cast his eyes round the walls and found them empty. He looked at his jacket—the number on the chest was almost rubbed off. That might be noticed. He ought to have it touched up. He ran his free hand over his chin and felt the stubble. His beard had grown fast since his last bath, over ten days back. But that didn't worry him. Next bath-day was about three days off and he'd have a shave then. What was the sense in queuing up at the barber's? Who did he have to doll himself up for?

Then as he eyed Vdovushkin's snow-white cap he remembered the hospital on the banks of the River Lovat where he'd been taken with a smashed jaw, and then—what a chump he was!— volunteered for the front again, though he could have lain there in bed for five days.

And now here he was dreaming of being ill for two or three weeks, not dangerously ill, of course, not so bad that they'd have to operate, yet bad enough to go to hospital and lie in bed for three weeks without stirring: and let them feed him on nothing but that clear soup of theirs, he wouldn't mind.

But, he recalled, now they didn't let you lie in bed even in the camp infirmary. A new doctor had arrived with one of the latest replenishments—Stepan Grigorych, a fussy, loud-voiced fellow who gave neither himself nor his patients any peace. He invented jobs in and around the infirmary for all the patients who could stand on their feet—fencing the garden, laying paths, bringing soil to the flowerbeds, and, in winter-time, erecting snow-barriers. Work, he said, was a first-rate medicine for any illness.

You can overwork a horse to death. That the doctor ought to understand. If *he*'d been sweating blood laying block's he'd quieten down, you could be sure of that.

Vdovushkin went on with his writing. He was, indeed, doing some work "on the side", but it was something beyond Shukhov's ken. He was making a fair copy of a long new poem that he'd finished the previous evening and had promised to show that day to Stepan Grigorych, the doctor who advocated work-therapy.

As can happen only in camps, Stepan Grigorych had advised Vdovushkin to describe himself as a medical assistant, and had taken him on at the infirmary and taught him to make intravenous injections on ignorant prisoners, to whose innocent minds it could never occur that Vdovushkin wasn't a medical assistant at all. Vdovushkin had been a university student of literature, arrested while still in his second year. The doctor wanted him to write when in prison what he'd been given no opportunity to write in freedom.

The signal for the muster was barely audible through the double-paned, frost-blurred windows. Shukhov heaved a sigh and stood up. He still had that feverish chill but evidently he wouldn't be able to skip work.

Vdovushkin reached for the thermometer and read it.

"H'm, neither one thing nor the other. Thirty-seven point two. If it had been thirty-eight it would have been clear to anyone. I can't exempt you. Stay behind at your own risk, if you like. The doctor will examine you. If he considers you're ill he'll exempt you. If he finds you fit, he won't. Then you'll be locked up. You'd do best to go to work."

Shukhov said nothing. He didn't even nod. Pulling his hat over his eyes, he walked out.

How can you expect a man who's warm to understand one who's cold?

The cold stung. A murky fog wrapped itself round Shukhov and made him cough painfully. The temperature out there was −27°; Shukhov's temperature was +37°. The fight was on.

He ran at a jog trot to his hut. The whole mustering-ground was deserted, the camp looked empty. It was that brief moment of relaxation when, although everything has been decided, everyone is pretending to himself that there will be no march to work. The sentries sit in warm quarters, their sleepy heads propped against their rifles—it's not all milk and honey for them either, lounging on the watch-towers in such cold. The guards at the main gate tossed coal into the stove. The camp-guards in their room smoked a last cigarette before searching the barracks. And the prisoners, now clad in all their rags, a cord round their waists, their faces bound from chin to eyes with bits of cloth against the cold, lay on their bunks with their boots on and waited, eyes shut, hearts aquake, for their team-leader to yell: "Out you get."

The 104th were dozing with the rest in Hut 7—all except Pavlo, the deputy team-leader, who moved his lips as he totted something up with a pencil, and Alyosha, Shukhov's clean and tidy neighbour, who was reading from a notebook in which he'd copied out half the New Testament.

Shukhov ran headlong, but without making any noise, straight to Pavlo's bunk.

Pavlo looked up.

"So they didn't put you in the lock-up, Ivan Denisovich? All right?" he asked with a marked Ukrainian accent, rolling out the name and patronymic in the way West Ukrainians did even in prison.

Picking up Shukhov's bread-ration he handed it to him. A spoonful of granulated sugar lay in a small mound on top of the hunk. Shukhov had no time to spare but he answered properly (the deputy team-leader was also one of the authorities, and even more depended on him than on the camp commandant). And, though he was in a hurry, he sucked the sugar from the bread with his lips, licked it under his tongue as he put his foot on a support to climb up to make his bed, and took a look at his ration, weighing it in his hand and hastily calculating whether it reached the regulation fivefifty grams. He had drawn many a thousand of these rations in prisons and camps, and though he'd never had an opportunity to weigh them on scales, and although, being a man of timid nature, he knew no way of standing up for his rights, he, like every other prisoner, had discovered long ago that honest weight was never to be found in the bread-cutting. There was short weight in every ration. The only point was how short. So every day you took a look to soothe your soul—today, maybe, they haven't snitched any.

He decided he was 20 grams short as he broke the bread in two. One half he stuck into his bosom, into a little clean pocket he'd specially sewn under his jacket (at the factory they make jackets for prisoners without pockets). The other half, which he'd saved by going without at breakfast, he considered eating on the spot.

But food gulped down is no food at all; it's wasted; it gives you no feeling of fullness. He made to put the bread into his locker but again thought better of it: he recalled that two barrack-orderlies had been beaten up for filching. The hut was a big place, like a public yard.

And so, still clutching the hunk of bread, he drew his feet out of his valenki, deftly leaving inside them his foot-cloths and spoon, crawled barefoot up to his bunk, widened a little hole in the mattress and there, amidst the sawdust, concealed his half-ration. He pulled off his hat, drew out of it a needle and thread (hidden deeply, for they fingered the hats when they frisked you; once a guard had pricked his finger and almost broken Shukhov's skull in his rage). Stitch, stitch, stitch, and the little tear in the mattress was mended, with the bread concealed under it. Meanwhile the sugar in his mouth had melted. Every nerve was strained to breaking-point. At any moment the roster-guard would begin shouting at the door. Shukhov's fingers worked fast but his mind, planning the next move, worked faster.

Alyosha the Baptist was reading the Testament under his breath (perhaps specially for Shukhov—those fellows were fond of recruiting):

"If you suffer, it must not be for murder, theft, or sorcery, nor for infringing the rights of others. But if anyone suffers as a Christian, he should feel it no disgrace, but confess that name to the honour of God."

Alyosha was smart: he'd made a chink in the wall and hidden the little book in it, and it had survived every search.

With the same rapid movements as before, Shukhov hung up his coat on a cross-beam and pulled what he wanted from under the mattress: a pair of mittens, a second pair of old foot-clothes, a length of cord and a piece of rag with tapes at each end. He smoothed the sawdust in the mattress (it was lumpy and dense), tucked in the blanket, arranged the pillow, and slid down on to his bare feet and started binding them with the cloths, first with the good ones, then, on top, with the torn.

Just then Tiurin stood up and barked:

"Sleep's over, One hundred and fourth! Out you get."

And at once the entire team, drowsing or not, got up, yawned, and went to the door. Tiurin had been in for nineteen years and never turned his men out for the muster a moment too soon. When he said "Out you get" it meant you'd better.

And while the men with heavy tread and tight lips walked into the corridor one by one and then on to the porch, and the leader of the 20th, following Tiurin's example, called in turn "Out you get", Shukhov drew his valenki over the double thickness of foot-cloths, slipped his coat over his wadded jacket and fastened a cord tightly round him (leather belts had been removed from zeks who had them—leather belts weren't allowed in "special" camps).

So Shukhov managed to get everything done and to catch up with the last of his companions, just as their numbered backs were passing through the door on to the porch. Looking rather bulky, for they had wrapped themselves up in every garment they possessed, the men shuffled diagonally towards the mustering-ground in single file, making no attempt to overtake one another. The only sound was the crunch of their heavy tread on the snow.

It was still dark, though in the east the sky was beginning to glow with a greenish tint. A light but piercing breeze came to meet them from the rising sun.

There is nothing as bitter as this moment when you go out to the morning muster—in the dark, in the cold, with a hungry belly, to face a whole day of work. You lose your tongue. You lose all desire to speak to anyone.

A junior guard was dashing about the mustering-ground.

"Well, Tiurin, how long do we have to wait for you? Late again?"

Maybe Shukhov might get scared of him but not Tiurin, oh no. He wouldn't waste breath on him in the cold. Just stumped on in silence.

And the team followed him through the snow. Shuffle, shuffle, squeak, squeak.

Tiurin must have greased them with that kilogram of pork-fat, for the 104th had gone back to its old place in the column—that could be seen from the neighbouring teams. So one of the poorer and stupider teams was being sent to the "Socialist Way of Life" settlement. Oh, it'd be cruel there today: twenty-seven degrees of frost, and windy. No shelter. No fire.

A team-leader needs a lot of pork-fat: to take to the planning department, and to satisfy his own belly too. Tiurin received no parcels but he didn't go short of fat. No one in the team who received any lost a moment in taking him some as a gift.

Otherwise you'd never survive.

The senior roster-guard glanced at a small piece of board.

"You have one away on sick-leave today, Tiurin. Twenty-three present?"

"Twenty-three," said Tiurin with a nod.

Who was missing? Panteleyev wasn't there. But surely he wasn't ill.

And at once a whisper ran through the team: Panteleyev, that son of a bitch, was staying behind again. Oh no, he wasn't ill, the security boys were keeping him back. He'd be peaching on someone.

They would send for him during the day, on the quiet, and keep him two or three hours. No one would see, no one would hear.

And they'd fix it all up with the medical authorities.

The whole mustering-ground was black with coats as the teams drifted forward to be searched. Shukhov remembered he wanted to have the numbers on his jacket touched up, and elbowed his way through the crowd to the side. Two or three prisoners stood waiting their turn with the artist. He joined them. They spelled nothing but trouble, those numbers: if they were distinct the guards could identify you from any distance, but if you neglected to have them repainted in time you'd be sure to land in the lock-up for not taking care of your number.

There were three artists in the camp. They painted pictures for the authorities free of charge, and in addition took it in turn to appear at the muster to touch up the numbers. Today it was the turn of an old man with a grey beard. When he painted the number on your hat with his brush it was just like a priest anointing your brow.

The old man painted on and on, blowing from time to time into his glove. It was a thin, knitted glove. His hand grew stiff with cold. He only just managed to paint the numbers.

He touched up the S 854 on Shukhov's jacket, and Shukhov, holding his waist-cord in his hand and without bothering to pull his coat round him—very soon he'd be frisked—caught up with the team. At once he noticed that his team-mate Tsezar was smoking, and smoking a cigarette, not a pipe. That meant he might be able to cadge a smoke. But he didn't ask straight away, he stood quite close up to Tsezar and, half turning, looked past him.

He looked past him and seemed indifferent, but he noticed that after each puff (Tsezar inhaled at rare intervals thoughtfully) a thin ring of glowing ash crept down the cigarette, reducing its length as it moved stealthily to the cigarette-holder.

Fetiukov, that jackal, had come up closer too and now stood opposite Tsezar, watching his mouth with blazing eyes.

Shukhov had finished his last pinch of tobacco and saw no prospects of acquiring any more before evening. Every nerve in his body was taut, all his longing was concentrated in that fag-end —which meant more to him now, it seemed, than freedom itself: but he would never lower himself like that Fetiukov, he would never look at a man's mouth.

Tsezar was a hotch-potch of nationalities: Greek, Jew, Gypsy— you couldn't make out which. He was still young. He'd made films. But he hadn't finished his first when they arrested him. He wore a dark, thick, tangled moustache. They hadn't shaved it off in the camp because that was the way he looked in the photograph in his dossier.

"Tsezar Markovich," slobbered Fetiukov, unable to restrain himself. "Give us a drag."

His face twitched with greedy desire.

Tsezar slightly raised the lids that drooped low over his black eyes and looked at Fetiukov. It was because he didn't want to be interrupted while smoking and asked for a drag that he had taken up a pipe. He didn't begrudge the tobacco, he resented the interruption in his chain of thought. He smoked to stimulate his mind and to set his ideas flowing. But the moment he lighted a cigarette he read in several pairs of eyes an unspoken plea for the fag-end.

Tsezar turned to Shukhov and said:

"Take it, Ivan Denisovich."

And with his thumb he pushed the smouldering fag-end out of the short amber holder.

Shukhov started (though it was exactly what he had expected of Tsezar) and gratefully hurried to take the fag-end with one hand, while slipping the other hand under it to prevent it from

22

dropping. He didn't resent the fact that Tsezar felt squeamish about letting him finish the cigarette in the holder (some had clean mouths, some had foul) and he didn't burn his hardened fingers as they touched the glowing end. The main thing was, he had cut out that jackal Fetiukov, and now could go on drawing in smoke until his lips were scorched. Mmm. The smoke crept and flowed through his whole hungry body, making his head and feet respond to it.

Just at that blissful moment he heard a shout:

"They're stripping us of our undershirts."

Such was a prisoner's life. Shukhov had grown accustomed to it. All you could do was to look out they didn't leap at your throat.

But why the undershirts? The camp commandant himself had issued them. No, something was wrong.

There were still teams ahead of them before it was their turn to be frisked. Everyone in the 104th looked about. They saw Lieutenant Volkovoi, the security chief, stride out of the staff quarters and shout something to the guards. And the guards who, when Volkovoi wasn't around, carried out the frisking perfunctorily, now flung themselves into their work with savage zeal.

"Unbutton your shirts," the sergeant shouted.

Volkovoi was as unpopular with the prisoners as with the guards—even the camp commandant was said to be afraid of him. God had named the rogue appropriately.[1] He was a wolf indeed, and looked it. He was dark, tall, with a scowl, very quick in his movements. He'd turn up from behind a hut with a "What's going on here?" There was no hiding from him. At first, in '49, he'd been in the habit of carrying a whip of plaited leather, as thick as his forearm. He was said to have used it for flogging in the cells. Or when the prisoners would be standing in a group near a hut at the evening count, he'd slink up from behind and lash out at someone's neck with a "Why aren't you standing in line, trash?" The men would dash away in a wave. Stung by the blow, his victim would put a hand to his neck and wipe away the blood, but he'd hold his tongue, for fear of the cells.

Now, for some reason, Volkovoi had stopped carrying his whip. When the weather was cold the guards were fairly lenient

[1] *Volk* means wolf in Russian.

23

in the morning, though not in the evening. The prisoners untied their belts, and flung their coats wide open. They advanced five abreast, and five guards stood waiting to frisk them. The guards slapped their hands down the belted jackets, ran over the right knee-pocket, the only one permitted by regulation, and, reluctant to pull off their gloves, felt any object that puzzled them, asking lazily: "What's that?"

What was there to look for on a prisoner at the morning muster? A knife? But knives weren't taken out of the camp, they were brought into it. In the morning they had to make certain a prisoner wasn't taking three kilograms of bread with him, meaning to escape with it. There was a time when they were so scared of the 200-gram hunks the prisoners took to eat with their dinner that each of the teams had to make a wooden case for carrying the whole ration, after collecting it, piece by piece, from the men. What they reckoned to gain by this stupidity was beyond imagining. More likely it was just another way of tormenting people, giving them something extra to worry about. It meant taking a nibble at your hunk, making your mark on it, so to say, and then putting it in the case: but anyway the pieces were as alike as two peas, they were all off the same loaf. During the march it preyed on your mind: you tortured yourself by imagining that somebody else's bit of the ration might get substituted for yours. Why, good friends quarrelled about it, even to the point of fighting! But one day three prisoners escaped in a lorry from the working-site and took one of those cases of bread with them. That brought the authorities to their senses: they chopped up all the boxes in the guard-room. Everyone carry his own hunk, they said.

At this first search they also had to make sure that no one was wearing civvies under the camp outfit. But, after all, every prisoner had had his civvies removed from him down to the very last garment, and they wouldn't be returned, they were told, until they'd served their terms. No one had served his term in this camp.

Sometimes the guards frisked you for letters that might have been sent through civilians. But if they were going to search every prisoner for letters they'd be messing about till dinner-time.

Volkovoi, however, had shouted that they were to search

24

for something, and so the guards peeled off their gloves, ordered everyone to untuck his jacket (where every little bit of barrack-room warmth was treasured) and unbutton his shirt. Then they strode up to run their paws over the zeks and find out whether any of them might have slipped on something against the rules. A prisoner was allowed to wear a shirt and an undershirt—he was to be stripped of anything else: such were Volkovoi's instructions, passed down the ranks by the prisoners. The teams that had been frisked earlier were in luck. Some of them had already been passed through the gates. But the rest had to bare their breasts. And anyone who had slipped on an extra garment had to take it off on the spot, out there in the cold.

That's how it started, but it resulted in a fine mix-up—a gap formed in the column, and at the gates the escort began shouting "Get a move on, get a move on." So when it was the turn of the 104th to be frisked they had to ease up a bit: Volkovoi told the guards to take the name of anyone who might be wearing extra garments—the culprits were to surrender them in person at the camp-stores that evening with a written explanation of how and why they had hidden the garments.

Shukhov was in regulation dress. Come on, paw me as hard as you like. There's nothing but my soul in my chest. But they made a note that Tsezar was wearing a flannel vest and that Buinovsky, it seemed, had put on a waist-coat or a cummerbund or something. Buinovsky, who'd been in the camp less than three months, protested. He couldn't get rid of his commander's habits.

"You've no right to strip men in the cold. You don't know Article Nine of the Criminal Code."

But they did have the right. They knew the code. You, chum, are the one who doesn't know it.

"You're not behaving like Soviet people," Buinovsky went on saying. "You're not behaving like communists."

Volkovoi had put up with the references to the criminal code but this made him wince and, like black lightning, he flashed:

"Ten days in the cells."

And aside to the sergeant:

"Starting from this evening."

They didn't like putting a man in the cells in the morning: it

25

meant the loss of his work for a whole day. Let him sweat blood in the meantime and be put in the cells in the evening.

The prison lay just over there, to the left of the mustering-ground. A brick building with two wings. The second wing had been added that autumn—there wasn't room enough in the first. The prison had eighteen cells besides those for solitary confinement which were fenced off. The entire camp was log-built except for that brick prison.

The cold had got under the men's shirts and now it was there to stay. All that wrapping-up had been in vain.

Shukhov's back was giving him hell. How he longed to be in bed in the infirmary, fast asleep! He wanted nothing else. Under the heaviest of blankets.

The zeks stood in front of the gates, buttoning their coats, tying a rope round their bellies. And from outside the escort shouted:

"Come on. Come on."

And from behind, the guard urged them on:

"Get along. Get along."

The first gate. The border zone. The second gate. Railings along each side near the guard-house.

"Halt!" shouted a sentry. Like a flock of sheep. "Form fives."

It was growing light. The escort's fire was burning itself out behind the guard-house. They always lit a fire before the prisoners were sent out to work—to keep themselves warm and be able to see more clearly while counting.

One of the gate-guards counted in a loud brisk voice:

"First. Second. Third. . . ."

And the prisoners, in ranks of five, separated from the rest and marched ahead, so that they could be watched from front and behind: five heads, five backs, ten legs.

A second gate-guard—a checker—stood at the next rail in silence, simply verifying the count.

And, besides, a lieutenant stood watching.

That was from the camp side.

A man is more precious than gold. If there was one head short when they got past the wire you had to replace it with your own.

Once more the team came together.

26

And now it was the turn of the sergeant of the escort to count. "First. Second. Third."

And each rank of five drew away and marched forward separately.

And on the other side of the wire the deputy head-guard verified the count.

And another lieutenant stood by and watched.

That was from the side of the escort.

No one dared make a mistake. If you signed for one head too many, you filled the gap with your own.

There were escort-guards all over the place. They flung a semicircle round the column on its way to the power-station, their tommy-guns sticking out and pointing right at your face. And there were guards with grey dogs. One dog bared its fangs as if laughing at the prisoners. The escorts all wore short sheepskins, except for half a dozen whose coats trailed the ground. The long sheepskins were interchangeable: they were worn by anyone whose turn had come to man the watch-towers.

And once again as they brought the teams together the escort recounted the entire power-station column by fives.

"You always get the sharpest frost at sunrise," said Buinovsky. "You see, it's the coldest point of the night."

Captain Buinovsky was fond of explaining things. The state of the moon—whether it was old or young—he could calculate it for any day of the year.

He was fading away under your very eyes, the captain, his cheeks were falling in. But he had pluck.

Out beyond the camp-boundary the intense cold, accompanied by a head wind, stung even Shukhov's face, which was used to every kind of unpleasantness. Realizing that he would have the wind in his face all the way to the power-station, he decided to make use of his bit of rag. To meet the contingency of a head wind he, like many other prisoners, had got himself a cloth with a long tape at each end. The prisoners admitted that these helped a bit. Shukhov covered his face up to the eyes, brought the tapes round below his ears, and fastened the ends together at the back of his neck. Then he covered his nape with the flap of his hat and raised his coat-collar. The next thing was to pull the front flap of the hat down on to his brow. Thus in front only his eyes remained unprotected. He fixed his coat tightly at the waist with the cord. Now everything was in order except for his hands, which were already stiff with cold (his mittens were wretched). He rubbed them, he clapped them together, for he knew that in a moment he'd have to put them behind his back and keep them there for the entire march.

The chief of the escort recited the "morning prayer", which every prisoner was heartily sick of:

"Attention, prisoners. Marching orders must be strictly obeyed. Keep to your ranks. No hurrying, keep a steady pace. No talking. Keep your eyes fixed ahead and your hands behind your backs. A step to right or left is considered an attempt to escape and the escort has orders to shoot without warning. Leading guards, quick march."

The two guards in the lead of the escort must have set out along the road. The column heaved forward, shoulders swaying, and the escorts, some twenty paces to the right and left of the column, each man at a distance of ten paces from the next, tommy-guns at the ready, set off too.

It hadn't snowed for a week and the road was worn hard and smooth. They skirted the camp and the wind caught their faces sideways. Hands clasped behind their backs, heads lowered, the column of prisoners moved on, as though at a funeral. All you saw was the feet of two or three men ahead of you and the patch of trodden ground where your own feet were stepping. From time to time one of the escorts would cry: "U 48. Hands behind back", or "B 502. Keep up." But they shouted less and less: the slashing wind made it difficult to see. The guards weren't allowed to tie cloth over their faces. Theirs was not much of a job either.

In warmer weather everybody in the column talked, no matter how much the escort might shout at them. But today every prisoner hunched his shoulders, hid behind the back of the man in front of him and plunged into his own thoughts.

The thoughts of a prisoner—they're not free either. They keep returning to the same things. A single idea keeps stirring. Would they feel that piece of bread in the mattress? Would he have any luck at the sick-bay that evening? Would they put Buinovsky in the cells? And how did Tsezar get his hands on that warm vest? He'd probably greased a palm or two in the store for people's private belongings. How else?

Because he had breakfasted without bread and eaten his food cold, Shukhov's belly felt unsatisfied that morning. And to prevent it complaining and begging for food, he stopped thinking about the camp and let his mind dwell on the letter he'd soon be writing home.

The column passed the wood-processing factory, built by prison labour, the workers' settlement (the huts had been assembled by prisoners too, but the inhabitants were civilians), the new club (convict-built in entirety, from the foundations to the mural decorations—but it wasn't they who saw the films there), and then moved out into the steppe, straight into the wind, heading for the reddening dawn. Bare white snow stretched to the horizon, to the left, to the right, and not a single tree could be seen on the whole expanse of steppe.

A new year, 1951, had begun, and Shukhov had the right to two letters that year. He had sent his last letter in July and got an answer to it in October. At Ust-Izhma the rules had been different: you could write once a month. But what was the sense of writing? He'd written no more often then than now.

Ivan Shukhov had left home on June 23, 1941. On the previous Sunday the people who'd been to Polomnya to attend Mass had said: *War!* At Polomnya they'd learned it at the post-office but at Temnenovo no one had a wireless in those days. Now, they wrote, it roared in every cottage—it was piped. There was as little sense in writing now as in casting a stone in some bottomless pool. It sinks, and that's the last you hear of it. You couldn't write and describe the team you were working with and what kind of team-leader Andrei Prokofievich was. Just now he had a good deal more to talk about with Kilgas the Lett than with his family at home.

Neither did the two letters a year they sent him throw much light on the way they were living. The kolkhoz had a new chairman—as if that hadn't happened regularly! It'd been amalgamated with neighbouring farms—that'd happened before, too, but afterwards they'd reduced it to its former condition. And what else? The farmers who were failing to fulfil their quota of work-days— or that the individual plots had been cut down to 1,500 square metres, and some people's right back to the cottage walls.

What he couldn't take in was the fact that, as his wife wrote, the number of people in the kolkhoz hadn't grown by a single soul since the war. All the young men and women, without exception, had contrived to get away to work in factories or in the peat-processing works. Half the men hadn't come back from the war at all and, among those who had, were some who cold-shouldered the kolkhoz. They lived in the village and worked on the side. The only men on the farm were Zakha Vasilych the team-leader and Tikhon the carpenter, who was turned eighty-four, had married recently and already had children. The kolkhoz was kept going by the women who'd been there since 1930.

There was something about this that Shukhov couldn't understand—"living in the village and working on the side." He'd seen life in the days of private farming and in the days of the kolkhozes too, but that men weren't working in their own villages—this he couldn't swallow. Sort of seasonal workers, were they? Going out travelling? But then how did the village manage with the haymaking?

They'd given up seasonal work a long time back, his wife had replied. They didn't go out carpentering, for which that part of the country was famous; they didn't make osier baskets, for no one wanted them these days. But they did have a craft, a new, jolly craft—carpet-painting. Someone had brought stencils back from the war and from that time the thing became popular and the number of those carpet-painters grew and grew. They had no steady jobs, they didn't work anywhere, they helped the kolkhoz for a month or so, just at the haymaking or the harvesting, and for that the kolkhoz gave them a chit saying that so-and-so, a member of the kolkhoz, had been released to carry on his work and that the kolkhoz had no claim on him. And they travelled all over the country, they even flew in aeroplanes to save time, and they piled up roubles by the thousand and painted carpets all over the place. Fifty roubles a carpet made out of any old sheet you could spare—and it didn't seem to take them more than an hour to make a carpet of it. And Shukhov's wife nursed the strong hope that when Ivan returned he too would become one of those painters. Then they'd raise themselves out of the poverty in which she was living and they'd send the children to a technical school and build a new cottage instead of the old rotten one. All the carpet-painters were building new cottages and now, near the railway station, the cottages had gone up in price from five thousand to all of twenty-five.

Then Shukhov asked his wife to explain to him how he, who'd never been able to draw in his life, was going to become a painter. And what were those beautiful carpets like? What did they have on them? His wife answered that you'd have to be an utter fool not to be able to paint the patterns; all you had to do was to put the stencil on and paint through the little holes with a brush. There were three sorts of carpets, she wrote: the "Troika", an officer of the hussars driving a beautiful *troika*; the "Reindeer"; and a third with a Persian-style pattern. They had no other designs, but people all over the country were glad to get these and snatch them out of the painters' hands. Because a real carpet cost not fifty but thousands of roubles.

How Shukhov longed to see just one of those carpets!

During his years in prisons and camps he'd lost the habit of planning for the next day, for a year ahead, for supporting his family. The authorities did his thinking for him about everything —it was somehow easier that way. He still had another two winters, another two summers to serve. But those carpets preyed on his mind. . . .

There was easy money to be made, you see, and made fast. And somehow it seemed a pity to lag behind his fellow-villagers. . . . But, candidly, he didn't want to turn carpet-painter. For that a man needed to be free-and-easy with people, to be brash, to know how to grease a palm or two. And although Shukhov had trodden the earth for forty years, though he'd lost half his teeth and his head was growing bald, he'd never either given or taken a bribe, nor had he learned to do so in camp.

Easy money weighs light in the hand and doesn't give you the feeling you've earned it. There was truth in the old saw: pay short money and get short value. He still had a good pair of hands, capable hands. Surely, when he was out, he'd find work as a stove-setter, a carpenter or tinker?

Only if they deprived him of his civil rights and he couldn't be taken on anywhere, or if they wouldn't let him go home, could he turn to those carpets for a spell.

Meanwhile the column had come to a halt before the guard-house of the great sprawling site on which the power-station stood. While the column was still on the move, two of the escort, clad in ankle-length sheepskins, had left their places and wandered across open country to their distant watch-towers. Until all the towers were manned the site was forbidden territory. The head-guard, a tommy-gun slung over his shoulder, advanced to the guard-house. Smoke, a great cloud of it, belched from its chimney: a civilian watchman sat there all night to prevent anyone filching planks or cement.

Far in the distance, on the other side of the site, the sun, red and enormous, was rising in haze, its beams cutting obliquely through the gates, the whole building-site and the fence. Alyosha, who was standing next to Shukhov, gazed at the sun and looked happy, a smile on his lips. What had he to be happy about? His cheeks were sunken, he lived strictly on his rations, he earned nothing. He spent all his Sundays muttering with the other Baptists. They shed the hardships of camp life like water off a duck's back.

During the march, Shukhov's face-cloth had grown quite wet from his breath. In some place the frost had caught it and formed an icy crust. He drew it down from his face to his neck and stood with his back to the wind. He'd managed to keep the cold out in most places, though his hands were numb in his worn mittens. The toes of his left foot were numb too: that left boot was badly worn. The sole had been repaired twice.

The small of his back ached, and so did the rest of it, all the way up to his shoulders. Ached and throbbed. How could he work?

He looked round, and his eyes fell on the face of the team-leader, who had marched among the last five. Tiurin was a broad-shouldered man, broad in the face too. He looked morose as he stood there. He had no jokes or smiles for his team, but he took pains to see they got better rations. He was serving his second term; he was a true son of the GULAG[1] and knew camp ways through and through.

In camp the team-leader is everything: a good one will give you a second life, a bad one will put you in your coffin. Shukhov

[1] Central Camp Administration: here used to mean camps in general.

32

had known Andrei Tiurin since the time they met at Ust-Izhma, though he hadn't been in his team then. And when the prisoners who were in under Article 58¹ were transferred from general camps to "special" ones, Tiurin had immediately picked him out for his team. Shukhov had no dealings with the camp commandant or the P.P.D., with foremen or engineers—that was the team-leader's job: he'd protect him with his own chest of steel. In return, Tiurin had only to lift an eyebrow or beckon with a finger —and you ran and did what he wanted. You can cheat anyone you like in camp, but not your team-leader. Then you'll live.

Shukhov would have liked to ask Tiurin whether they were to work at the same place as the day before or go somewhere else, but he was afraid to interrupt his lofty thoughts. He'd only just averted the danger of the team being sent to work at the Socialist Way of Life settlement, and now he was probably deliberating over the "percentage"² on which the team's rations for the next five days depended.

Tiurin was heavily pock-marked. He was facing the wind but not a muscle moved—his skin was as tough as the bark of an oak.

In the column, the prisoners were clapping their hands and stamping their feet. The wind was nasty. It looked now as if the sentries, known to the prisoners as "parrots", were perched in all six watch-towers, but still they weren't letting the column in. They badgered the life out of you with their vigilance.

Here they are. The head-guard came out of the watch-house with the work-checker. They posted themselves on each side of the gate. The gates swung wide open.

"Form fives. First. Second. Third. . . ."

The prisoners marched as though on parade, almost in step. To get inside, that was all they wanted—there no one had to teach them what to do.

Just beyond the guard-house was the office: near it stood the works-superintendent, beckoning the team-leaders to turn in at it, not that they didn't head that way anyway. Der, too, was there, a convict himself but a foreman, the swine, who treated his fellow-prisoners worse than dogs.

¹ For political crimes.
² A paper stating the amount of work done and the percentage of the plan it amounts to.

33

Eight o'clock. Five minutes past (the hooter had just gone for the hour). The authorities were afraid that the prisoners might waste time and scatter into warm corners—and the prisoners had a long day ahead of them, there was time enough for everything. Everyone who steps on to the building-site bends to pick up a scrap of firewood here and there—fuel for the stove. And they hoard it away in nooks and crannies.

Tiurin ordered Pavlo to go with him to the office. Tsezar turned in there too. Tsezar was well off. Two parcels a month. He greased every palm that had to be greased, and worked in the office in a cushy job, as assistant to the norm-checker.

The rest of the team at once turned off to the side and beat it.

The sun rose red and hazy over the deserted area. At one place the panels of the prefabs lay under the snow; at another a start had been made on the brickwork, and abandoned when no higher than the foundations. Here lay a broken excavator-lever, there a scoop, further on a pile of scrap-metal. A network of ditches and trenches criss-crossed the site with a pit or two here and there. The building of the automobile repair-shop was ready for roofing. On a rise stood the power-station itself, built up to the second storey.

Now there was not a soul in sight. Only the six sentries on their watch-towers were visible—and some people bustling round the office. That moment belonged to the prisoners. The senior works-superintendent, it was said, had long been threatening to save time by giving the teams their work-rosters the evening before, but for all his efforts they never got round to it—because between the evening and the following morning all their plans turned upside down.

So that moment still belonged to the prisoners. While the authorities were sorting things out you stuck to the warmest place you could find. Sit down, take a rest, you'll have time enough to sweat blood. Good if you can get near a stove. Unwrap your foot-cloths and warm them a little. Then your feet will keep warm all day. And even without a stove it's good to sit down.

The 104th went into a big room in the repair-shop where the windows had been glazed during the autumn and the 38th were pouring slabs of concrete. Some of the slabs lay in moulds, others, with mesh reinforcement, were stood up on end. The ceiling was high, the floor was of bare earth: a cold place it would've been if they hadn't heated it with lots of coal—not for the sake of the men working there, of course, but to help the slabs set faster. There was even a thermometer, and on Sundays, if for some reason or other no one was sent from the camp to work there, a civilian kept the stove going.

The 38th, naturally, wouldn't let any stranger near their stove. Their own men sat round it, drying their foot-cloths. Never mind, we'll sit here in the corner, it's not so bad.

Shukhov found a place for the seat of his wadded trousers—where hadn't they sat?—on the edge of a wooden mould, and leaned against the wall. When he did so his coat and jacket tightened, and he felt something sharp pressing against the left side of his chest, near his heart. It was the edge of the hunk of bread in his little inner pocket—that half of his morning ration which he'd taken with him for dinner. He always brought the same amount with him to work and never touched it till dinner-time. But usually he ate the other half at breakfast. This time he hadn't. But he realized he had gained nothing by economising: his belly called out to him to eat the bread at once, in the warmth. Dinner was five hours off—and time dragged.

And that nagging pain had now moved down to his legs, which felt quite weak. Oh, if he could only get to the stove!

He laid his mittens on his knees, unbuttoned his coat, untied the tapes of his face-cloth, stiff with cold, folded it several times over and put it away in his knee-pocket. Then he reached for the hunk of bread, wrapped in a piece of clean cloth, and, holding the cloth at chest level so that not a crumb should fall to the ground, began to nibble and chew at the bread. The bread, which he had carried under two garments, had been warmed by his body. The frost hadn't caught it at all.

More than once during his life in the camps, Shukhov had recalled the way they used to eat in his village: whole saucepans of potatoes, pots of porridge and, in the early days, big chunks of meat. And milk enough to split their guts. That wasn't the way to eat, he learned in camp. You had to eat with all your mind on the food—like now, nibbling the bread bit by bit, working the crumbs up into a paste with your tongue and sucking it into your cheeks. And how good it tasted, that soggy black bread! What had he eaten for eight, no, more than eight years? Next to nothing. But how much work had he done? Ah!

So he sat there, occupying himself with his hunk of bread, while near him on the same side of the room sat the rest of the 104th.

Two Estonians, close as brothers, sat on a flat concrete panel taking turns to smoke half a cigarette from the same holder. These Estonians were equally fair, equally tall, equally lean, and had equally long noses and big eyes. They hung on to each other so closely that you'd think one would suffocate unless he breathed the same air as the other. Tiurin never separated them. They shared their food, they slept in adjacent bunks in the top row. And when they stood in the column, waiting for work to start, or turned in for the night, they went on talking to each other in their quiet, deliberate manner. In fact they weren't brothers at all. They first met here in the 104th. One of them, they explained, had been a fisherman on the coast, the other had been taken as a child to Sweden by his parents when the Soviets were established in Estonia. But he'd grown up with a mind of his own and returned to Estonia to complete his education.

Well, it's said that nationality doesn't mean anything and that every nation has its bad eggs. But among all the Estonians Shukhov had known he'd never met a bad one.

The prisoners sat round, some on the panels, some on moulds, some straight on the ground. A tongue doesn't wag in the morning; everyone sat silent, locked in thought. Fetiukov, the jackal, had been collecting fag-ends (he even fished them out of the spittoons, he wasn't fussy), and now he was breaking them up and filtering the unsmoked tobacco on to a piece of paper. Fetiukov had three children at home but when he was sentenced they'd disclaimed him and his wife had married again. So he got no help from anywhere.

Buinovsky, who kept stealing glances at him, finally barked:

"Hey, you, what d'you think you're doing? Picking up all kinds of infection? You'll get a syphilitic lip that way. Stop it."

The captain was used to giving orders. He spoke to everyone as if in command.

But Fetiukov didn't give a damn for him—the captain got no parcels either. And with a malicious grin on his drooling lips he replied:

36

"You wait, captain. When you've been in for eight years you'll be picking them up yourself. We've seen prouder ones than you in the camp. . . ."

Fetiukov was judging by his own standards. Perhaps the captain would stand up to camp life.

"What? What?" asked Senka Klevshin, missing the point. Senka was deaf and thought they were talking about Buinovsky's bad luck during the frisking. "You shouldn't have shown your pride so much," he said, shaking his head in commiseration. "It could all have blown over."

Senka was a quiet, luckless fellow. One of his ear-drums had been smashed in '41. Then he was captured; he escaped, was recaptured, and was sent to Buchenwald. There he evaded death by a miracle and now he was serving his time here quietly. If you show your pride too much, he said, you're lost.

There was truth in that. Better to growl and submit. If you were stubborn they broke you.

Alyosha sat silent, his face buried in his hands. Praying.

Shukhov ate his bread down to his very fingers, keeping only a little bit of bare crust, the half-moon-shaped top of the loaf—because no spoon is as good for scraping a bowl of porridge clean as a bread-crust. He wrapped the crust in his cloth and slipped it into his inside pocket for dinner, buttoned himself up against the cold and prepared for work. Let them send him out now! Though, of course, it would be better if they'd wait a bit longer.

The 38th stood up and scattered—some to the concrete-mixer, some to fetch water, some to the reinforcement-meshes.

But neither Pavlo nor Tiurin came to their team. And although the 104th had been sitting there barely twenty minutes and the working-day—curtailed because it was winter—didn't end till six, everyone felt already they'd had a rare stroke of luck—now evening didn't seem so far off.

"Ekh, it's a long time since we had a snowstorm," said Kilgas, a plump, red-faced Lett, gesturing. "Not one snow-storm all winter. What sort of winter d'you call this?"

"Yes . . . a snowstorm . . . a snowstorm," the team sighed in response.

When there was a snowstorm in those parts no one was taken out to work: they were afraid of letting the prisoners leave the

37

barracks. They could get lost between the barrack-room and the mess-hall if you didn't put up a guide rope. No one would care if a prisoner froze to death, but what if he tried to escape? There had been instances. During the storms the snow was as fine as dust but the drifts were as firm as ice. Prisoners had escaped over them when they topped the barbed wire. True, they hadn't got far.

Come to think of it, a snowstorm was no use to anyone. The prisoners sat locked in; the coal was delivered late and all the warmth was blown out of the hut. Flour didn't reach the camp, so there was no bread; and more often than not there was no hot food either. And as long as the storm lasted—three days, four days, even a week—those days were reckoned as holidays and had to be made up for by work on Sunday.

All the same, the prisoners loved snowstorms and prayed for them. Whenever the wind rose a little, every face was turned up to the sky: Let the stuff come! The more the merrier.

Snow, they meant. With only a ground wind, it never really got going.

Someone edged up to the stove of the 38th, only to be ousted.

Just then Tiurin walked in. He looked gloomy. His team understood that there was something to be done, and quickly.

"H'm," said Tiurin, looking round. "All present, hundred and fourth?"

He didn't verify or count them because none of Tiurin's men could have gone anywhere. Without wasting time he gave his men their assignments. The two Estonians, Senka and Gopchik, were sent to pick up a big wooden box for mixing mortar from near at hand and carry it to the power-station. They all immediately knew that they were being transferred to the half-completed building where work had been abandoned in the late autumn. The other men were sent with Pavlo to get tools. Four were ordered to shovel snow near the power-station and the entrance to the machine-room, and inside and on the ramps. A couple of men were sent to light the stove in the machine-room, using coal and such planks as they could pinch and chop up. Another was to drag cement there on a sledge. Two were sent to fetch water, two for sand, and yet another to sweep the snow off the sand and break it up with a crowbar.

The only two left without assignments were Shukhov and Kilgas, the leading workers of the team. Calling them over, Tiurin said;

"Well, look here, boys" (he was no older than they were but he had the habit of addressing them like that). "After dinner you'll be laying slag-blocks on the second-storey walls, over there where the 6th stopped work last autumn. Now we have to figure how to make the machine-room warmer. It has three big windows and the first thing to do is to board them up somehow. I'll give you people to help, but you must think what to board them up with. We're going to use the machine-room for mixing the mortar, and for warming ourselves too. Unless we keep warm we'll freeze like dogs, understand?"

He'd have said more, maybe, but up came Gopchik, a Ukrainian lad, pink as a sucking-pig, to complain that the other team wouldn't give them the box. There was a scrap going on over it. So off went Tiurin.

Difficult as it was to start working in such cold, the important thing was to get going.

Shukhov and Kilgas exchanged looks. They'd worked in a pair more than once as carpenter and mason, and had come to respect one another.

It was no easy matter to find something to board up those windows with in the bare expanse of snow. But Kilgas said:

"Vanya, I know a little place over there where those prefabs are going up, with a fine roll of roofing-felt. I put it aside with my own hands. Let's go and scrounge it."

Kilgas was a Lett but he spoke Russian like a native. There'd been a settlement of Old Believers near his village and he'd learned Russian from childhood. He'd been in the camp only two years but already he understood everything: if you don't use your teeth you get nothing. His name was Johann and Shukhov called him Vanya.

They decided to go for the roll: but first Shukhov ran over to where a new wing of the repair-shops was under construction. He had to get his trowel. For a mason a trowel is a serious matter—if it's light and easy to handle. But there was a rule that wherever you worked you had to turn in every evening the tools you'd been issued with that morning; and which tool you got the next day was a matter of chance. One evening, though, Shukhov had fooled the man in the tool-store and pocketed the best trowel; and now he kept it hidden in a different place every evening, and every morning, if he was put to laying blocks, he recovered it. If the 104th had been sent to the Socialist Way of Life settlement that morning Shukhov would of course have been without a trowel again. But now he had only to push aside a brick, dig his fingers into the chink—and hey presto! there it was.

Shukhov and Kilgas left the repair-shops and walked over towards the prefabs. Their breath formed thick clouds of vapour. The sun was now some way above the horizon but it cast no rays, as in a fog. On each side of it rose pillars of light.

"Like poles, eh?" Shukhov said with a nod.

"It's not poles we have to worry about," said Kilgas casually, "so long as they don't put any of that barbed-wire between them."

He never spoke without making a joke, that Kilgas, and was popular with the whole team for it. And what a reputation he had already won for himself among the Letts in the camp! Of course, it was true he ate properly—he received two food-parcels a month—and looked as ruddy as if he wasn't in camp at all. *You*'d make jokes if you were in his shoes!

This construction-site covered an immense area. It took quite a long time to cross it. On their way they ran into lads from the 82nd. Again they'd been given the job of pecking out holes in the ground. The holes were small enough—half a metre by half a metre and about the same in depth—but the ground, stone-hard even in summer, was now in the grip of frost. Just try and gnaw it! They went for it with picks—the picks slipped, scattering showers of sparks, but not a bit of earth was dislodged. The men stood there, one to a hole, and looked about them—nowhere to warm up, they were forbidden to budge a step—so back to the pick. The only way to keep warm.

Shukhov recognized one of them, a fellow from Viatka.

"Listen, navvy," he advised him. "You'd do better to light a fire over each hole. The ground would thaw out then.'

"It's forbidden," said the man. "They don't give us any fire-wood."

"Scrounge some then."

Kilgas merely spat.

"How d'you figure it, Vanya? If the authorities had any gumption, d'you think they'd put men on to pecking away at the ground with pickaxes in a frost like this?"

He muttered a few indistiguishable oaths and fell silent. You don't talk much in such cold. They walked on and on till they reached the spot where the panels of the prefabs lay buried under snow.

Shukhov liked to work with Kilgas. The only bad thing about him was that he didn't smoke and there was never any tobacco in his parcels.

Kilgas was right: together they lifted a couple of planks and there lay the roll of roofing-felt.

They lugged it out. Now, how were they going to carry it? They'd be spotted from the watch-towers, but that didn't matter: the "parrot's" only concern was that the prisoners shouldn't escape. Inside, you could chop up all those panels into firewood for all he cared. Nor would it matter if they happened to meet one of the guards. He'd be looking about like the others to see what he could scrounge. As for the prisoners, they didn't give a hoot for those prefabs, and neither did the team-leaders. The only people who kept an eye on them were the superintendent, who was a civilian, that swine Der, and the lanky Shkuropatenko, a mere cipher, a trusty who'd been given the temporary job of guarding the prefabs from any pilfering by the prisoners. Yes, it was Shkuropatenko who was most likely to spot them on the open ground.

"Look here, Vanya," said Shukhov, "we mustn't carry it flatways. Let's take it up on end with our arms round it. It'll be easy to carry and our bodies will hide it. They won't spot it from a distance."

It was a good idea. To carry the roll flatways would have been awkward, so they held it upright in between them and set off. From a distance it would look as if there were three of them, rather close to one another.

"But when Der notices the felt on the windows he'll guess where it came from," said Shukhov.

"What's it got to do with us?" asked Kilgas, in surprise. "We'll say it was there beforehand. Were we to pull it down or what?"

That was true.

41

Shukhov's fingers were numb with cold under his worn mittens. He'd lost all sense of touch. But his left boot was holding: that was the main thing. The numbness would go out of his fingers when he started to work.

They crossed the stretch of virgin snow and reached a sledge-trail running from the tool-store to the power-station. Their lads must have brought the cement along there.

The power-station stood on a rise at the edge of the site. No one had been near the place for weeks and the approaches to it lay under a smooth blanket of snow: the sledge tracks, and the fresh trails that had been left by the deep footsteps of the 104th, stood out boldly. The men were already clearing away the snow from round the building with wooden shovels and making a road for the lorries to drive up on.

It would have been good if the mechanical hoist in the power-station had been in order. But the motor had burned out, and no one had bothered to repair it. This meant that everything would have to be carried by hand to the second storey—the mortar and the blocks.

For two months the unfinished structure had stood in the snow like a grey skeleton, just as it had been left. And now the 104th had arrived. What was it that kept their spirits up? Empty bellies, fastened tight with belts of rope! A splitting frost! Not a warm corner, not a spark of fire! But the 104th had arrived—and life had come back to the building.

Right at the entrance to the machine-room the trough for mixing mortar fell apart. It was a ramshackle affair, and Shukhov hadn't expected it to last the journey in one piece. Tiurin swore at his men just for form's sake, for he saw that no one was to blame. At that moment Kilgas and Shukhov turned up with their roll of roofing-felt. Tiurin was delighted, and at once worked out a new arrangement: Shukhov was put to fixing the stove-pipe, so that a fire could be quickly kindled; Kilgas was to repair the mixing-box, with the two Estonians to help him; and Senka was given an axe to chop long laths with—felt could then be tacked to them, two widths for each window. Where were the laths to come from? Tiurin looked round. Everybody looked round. There was only one solution: to remove a couple of planks that served as a sort of handrail on the ramp leading up to the second storey. You'd have to keep your eyes skinned going up and down, otherwide you'd be over the edge. But where else were the planks to come from?

Why, you might wonder, should prisoners wear themselves out, working hard, ten years on end, in the camps? You'd think they'd say: No thank you, and that's that. We'll shuffle through the day till evening, and then the night is ours.

But that didn't work. To outsmart you they thought up work-teams—but not teams like the ones in freedom, where every man is paid his separate wage. Everything was so arranged in the camp that the prisoners egged one another on. It was like this: either you all got a bit extra or you all croaked. You're slacking, you rat—d'you think I'm willing to go hungry just because of you? Put your guts into it, scum.

And if a situation like this one turned up there was all the more reason for resisting the temptation to slack. Willy-nilly you put your back into the work. For unless you could manage to provide yourself with the means of warming up, you and everyone else would peg out on the spot.

Pavlo brought the tools. Now use them. A few lengths of stove-pipe, too. True, there were no tinsmith's tools but there was a little hammer and a light axe. One could manage.

Shukhov clapped his mittens together, joined up the lengths, and hammered the ends into the joints. He clapped his hands together again and repeated his hammering (he'd hidden his trowel in a nearby cranny. Although he was among his own lads one of them might swap it for his own. That applied to Kilgas too).

And then every thought was swept out of his head. All his memories and worries faded. He had only one idea—to fix the bend in the stove-pipe and hang it up to prevent it smoking. He sent Gopchik for a length of wire—hang up the pipe near the window with it, that would be best.

In the corner there was another stove, a squat one with a brick chimney. It had an iron plate on top that grew red-hot, and sand was to be thawed and dried on it. This stove had already been lit, and the captain and Fetiukov were bringing up barrows of sand. You don't have to be very bright to carry a hand-barrow. So the team-leader gave such work to people who'd been in positions of authority. Fetiukov had been a big shot in some office, with a car at his disposal.

43

At first Fetiukov had spat on the captain, bawled at him. But one sock on the jaw was enough. They got on all right after that.

The men bringing in the sand were sidling to the stove to warm up, but Tiurin drove them off.

"Look out, one of you is going to catch it in a jiffy. Wait till we've got the place fixed up.'

You've only to show a whip to a beaten dog. The frost was severe, but not as severe as the team-leader. The men scattered and went back to their jobs.

And Shukhov heard Tiurin say to Pavlo:

"Stay here and keep them at it. I'm going to hand in the work-report."

More depended on the work-report than on the work itself. A clever team-leader was one who concentrated on the work-report. That was what kept the men fed. He had to prove that work which hadn't been done had been done, to turn jobs that were rated low into ones that were rated high. For this a team-leader had to have his head screwed on, and to be on the right side of the checkers. Their palms had to be greased, too. But who benefited, then, from all those work-reports? Let's be clear about it. The camp. The camp got thousands of extra roubles from the building organization and so could give higher bonuses to its guard-lieutenants, such as to Volkovoi for using his whip. And you? You got an extra 200 grams of bread for your supper. A couple of hundred grams ruled your life.

Two buckets of water were carried in, but they had frozen on the way. Pavlo decided that there was no sense in doing it like this. Quicker to melt snow. They stood the buckets on the stove.

Gopchik brought along some new aluminium wire, used for electric leads.

"Ivan Denisovich," he said, as he turned it over to Shukhov, "it's good for making spoons. Teach me how to cast them."

Shukhov was fond of the scamp. His own son had died young, and the two daughters he had left at home were grown up. Gopchik had been arrested for taking milk to the forest for Bendera's men,[1] and had been given an adult's term of imprisonment. He was like a fawning puppy and he fawned on everyone.

[1] General in the Soviet Army who betrayed his country in World War II

44

But he'd already learned cunning: he ate the contents of his food-parcels alone, sometimes during the night.

After all, you couldn't feed everyone.

They broke off a length of wire for the spoons and hid it in a corner. Shukhov knocked together a couple of planks into a step-ladder and sent Gopchik up to hang the stove-pipe. The lad, as nimble as a squirrel, clambered up into the beams, knocked in a nail or two, slipped the wire round them, and passed it under the pipe. Shukhov didn't begrudge him his energy: he'd made another bend in the pipe close to the end. Though there was little wind that day there might be plenty tomorrow and this bend would prevent the pipe from smoking. They mustn't forget that it was for themselves that they were fixing the stove.

Meanwhile, Senka had finished making the laths, and Gopchik was again given the job of nailing them up. The little devil crept about up aloft, shouting down to the men.

The sun had risen higher, dispersing the haze. The two bright columns had gone. It was reddish inside the room. And now some-one had got the stove going with the filched wood. Made you feel a bit more cheerful.

"In January the sun warmed the flanks of the cow," Shukhov chanted.

Kilgas finished nailing the mortar-box together and, giving it an extra smash with his axe, shouted:

"Listen, Pavlo, I'll not take less than a hundred roubles from Tiurin for this job."

"You get a hundred grams," said Pavlo with a laugh.

"The prosecutor will make up the difference," shouted Gopchik from above.

"Stop that," Shukhov shouted, "stop". That wasn't the way to cut the roofing-felt.

He showed them how to do it.

The men crept up to the stove only to be chased away by Pavlo. He gave Kilgas some wood to make hods, for carrying the mortar up to the second storey. He put a couple more men on to bringing up the sand, others on to sweeping the snow off the scaffolding where the blocks were to be laid, and another on to taking the hot sand off the top of the stove and throwing it into the mortar-box.

A lorry-engine snorted outside. They were beginning to deliver

45

the blocks. The first lorry had got through. Pavlo hurried out and waved on the driver to where the blocks were to be dumped.

They put up one thickness of roofing-felt, then a second. What protection could you expect from it? It was paper, just paper. All the same, it looked like a kind of solid wall. The room became darker, and this brightened the stove up.

Alyosha brought in some coal. Some of them shouted to tip it on to the stove, others not to. They wanted to warm up with the flames. Alyosha hesitated, not knowing whom to obey.

Fetiukov had found himself a cosy corner near the stove and, the fool, was holding his boots right up to the flames. The captain took him by the scruff of the neck and lugged him off to the barrow.

"You shift sand, you louse."

The captain might still have been on board ship: if you were told to do something you did it. He had grown haggard during the past month, but he kept his bearing.

In the end all three windows were covered. Now the only light came through the door. And with it came the cold. So Pavlo had the upper half of the doorway boarded up but the lower left free, so that the men, by stooping, might get through it.

Meanwhile three lorries had driven up and dumped their loads of blocks. Now the problem was how to get the blocks up without a mechanical hoist.

"Masons, let's go and look round," Pavlo called.

It was a job to be respected. Shukhov and Kilgas went up with Pavlo. The ramp was narrow enough anyhow, but now that Senka had robbed it of its rails you must see that you pressed close to the wall if you weren't going to fall off it. And still worse—the snow had frozen to the treads and rounded them: they offered no grip to your feet. How would they bring up the mortar?

They looked all around to find where the blocks should be laid. The men Pavlo had sent up were shovelling the snow from the top of the walls. Here was the place. You had to take an axe to the ice on the old workings, and then sweep them clean.

They figured out how best to bring up the blocks. They looked down. They decided that, rather than carry them up the ramp, four men should be posted down below to heave the blocks up to that platform over there, that another couple should shift them on, and that two more should hand them up to the second storey. That would be quicker than carrying them up the ramp.

The wind wasn't strong but you felt it. It would pierce them all right when they started laying. They'd have to keep behind the bit of wall that the old lot had begun on, it would give them some shelter. Not too bad, it'd be warmer that way.

Shukhov looked up at the sky and gasped: it was clear that the sun had climbed almost to the dinner-hour. Wonder of wonders! How time flew when you were working! That was something he'd often noticed. The days rolled by in the camp—they were over before you could say "knife". But the years, they never rolled by: they never moved by a second.

When they went down, they found that everyone had settled round the stove except the captain and Fetiukov, who were still shifting sand. Pavlo flew into a rage and sent eight men out at once to move blocks, two to seep cement into the box and mix it with sand, another for water, another for coal. But Kilgas gave his own orders:

"Well, lads, we must finish with the barrows."

"Shall I give 'em a hand?" Shukhov volunteered.

"Yes, help them out," said Pavlo with a nod.

Just then they brought in a tank for melting snow. Someone had told the men that it was already noon.

Shukhov confirmed this.

"The sun's already reached its peak," he announced.

"If it's reached its peak," said the captain reflectively, "it's one o'clock, not noon."

"What do you mean?" Shukhov demurred. "Every greybeard knows that the sun stands highest at dinner-time."

"Greybeards, maybe," snapped the captain. "But since their day a new decree has been passed, and now the sun stands highest at one."

"Who passed that decree?"

"Soviet power."

The captain went out with a barrow. Anyway, Shukhov wouldn't have argued with him. Mean to say that even the sun in the heavens must kow-tow to their decrees?

The sound of hammering continued as the men knocked together four hods.

47

"All right, sit down for a bit and warm yourselves," said Pavlo to the two masons. "And you too, Senka. You can join them up there after dinner. Sit down."

So now they sat by the stove as of right. Anyway they couldn't start laying the blocks before dinner and there was no point in carrying the mortar up there—it would freeze.

The coals were gradually glowing red-hot and throwing out a steady heat. But you felt it only when you were near them—everywhere else the shop was as cold as ever.

They took off their mittens. All four men held their hands up to the stove.

But you never put your feet near the flame if you're wearing boots. You have to remember that. If they're leather boots the leather cracks, and if they're valenki the felt becomes sodden and begins to steam and you don't feel any warmer. And if you hold them still nearer the flame then they scorch, and you'll have to trail along till the spring with a hole in your boot—getting another pair can't be counted on.

"What does Shukhov care?" Kilgas said. "Shukhov, brothers, has one foot almost home."

"The bare one," said someone. They laughed (Shukhov had taken his mended boot off and was warming his foot-cloths).

"Shukhov's term's nearly up."

They'd given Kilgas twenty-five years. Earlier there'd been a spell when people were lucky: everyone to a man got ten years. But from '49 onwards the standard sentence was twenty-five, irrespective. A man can survive ten years—but twenty-five, who can get through alive?

Shukhov rather enjoyed having everybody poke a finger at him as if to say: Look at him, his term's nearly up. But he had his doubts about it. Those zeks who finished their time during the war had all been "retained pending special instructions" and had been released only in '46. Even those serving three-year sentences were kept for another five. The law can be stood on its head. When your ten years are up they can say "Here's another ten for you." Or exile you.

Yet there were times when you thought about it and you almost choked with excitement: Yes, your term really *is* coming to an end:

the bobbin is unwinding. . . . Good God! To step out to freedom, just walk out on your feet.

But it wasn't right for an old-timer to talk about it aloud, and Shukhov said to Kilgas:

"Don't you fret about those twenty-five years of yours. It's none so sure you'll be in all that time. But that I've been in eight full years, that's a fact."

Aye, you live with your mug in the mire and there's no time to be thinking about how you got in or how you're going to get out.

According to his dossier, Ivan Denisovich Shukhov had been sentenced for high treason. He had testified to it himself. Yes, he'd surrendered to the Germans with the intention of betraying his country and he'd returned from captivity to carry out a mission for German intelligence. What sort of mission neither Shukhov nor the interrogator could say. So it had been left at that—a mission.

Shukhov reckoned simply. If he didn't sign he'd be shot. If he signed he'd still get a chance to live. So he signed.

But what really happened was this. In February 1942 their whole army was surrounded on the north-west front. No food was parachuted to them. There were no planes. Things got so bad that they were scraping the hooves of dead horses—the horn could be soaked in water and eaten. They'd no ammunition left. So the Germans rounded them up in the forest, a few at a time. Shukhov was in one of these groups, and remained in German captivity for a day or two. Then five of them managed to escape. They stole through the forest and marshes again, and, by a miracle, reached their own lines. A tommy-gunner shot two of them on the spot, a third died of his wounds, but two got through. Had they been wiser they'd have said they'd been wandering about the forest, and then nothing would have happened. But they told the truth: they said they were escaped p.o.w.s. P.o.w.s, you ——! If all five of them had got through, their statements could have been found to tally and they might have been believed. But with two it was hopeless. You've put your bloody heads together and cooked up that escape story, they were told.

Deaf though he was, Senka caught on that they were talking about escaping from the Germans, and said in a loud voice:

"Three times I escaped, and three times they caught me."

Senka, who had suffered so much, was usually silent: he didn't hear what people said and didn't mix in their conversation. Little was known about him, only that he'd been in Buchenwald, where he'd worked with the underground and smuggled in arms for the mutiny: and how the Germans had punished him by tying his wrists behind his back, hanging him up by them, and flogging him.

"You've been in for eight years, Vanya," Kilgas argued. "But what camps? Not 'specials'. You had women to sleep with. You didn't wear numbers. But try and spend eight years in a 'special'— doing hard labour. No one's come out of a 'special' alive."

"Women! Logs, not women."

Shukhov stared at the coals in the stove and remembered his seven years in the north. And how he worked for three years hauling logs—for packing-cases and sleepers.

The flames in the camp fires had danced up there, too—at timber-felling during the night. Their chief made it a rule that any team that had failed in its quota had to stay in the forest after dark.

They'd toil back to the camp in the early hours but had to be in the forest again next morning.

"N-no, brothers . . . I think we have a quieter life here," he lisped. "Here, when the shift's over, we go back to the camp whether our stint's done or not. That's a law. And bread—a hundred grams more, basic, than up there. Here a man can live. All right, it's a 'special' camp. So what? Does it bother you to wear a number? They don't weigh anything, those numbers."

"A quieter life, d'you call it?" Fetiukov hissed (the dinner-break was getting near and everyone was huddling round the stove). "Men having their throats cut, in their bunks! And you call it quieter!"

"Not men—squealers." Pavlo raised a threatening finger at Fetiukov.

True enough, something new had started up. Two men, known to be squealers, had been found in their bunks one morning with their throats cut; and, a few days later, the same thing had happened to an innocent zek—someone must have gone to the wrong bunk. And one squealer had run off on his own to the chief of the lock-up and they'd put him inside for safety. Amazing. . . . Nothing like that had happened in the ordinary camps. Nor here, either, up till then.

Suddenly the hooter went. It never began at full blast. It started hoarsely, as though clearing its throat.

Mid day. Down tools. The dinner-break.

Ekh, they'd left it too late. They should have gone off to the canteen long ago and taken their places in the queue. There were eleven teams at work at the power-station and there was room in the canteen for only two at a time.

Tiurin was still missing. Pavlo cast a rapid glance round the shop and said:

"Shukhov and Gopchik, you come with me. Kilgas, as soon as I send Gopchik to you, bring the whole team along."

Others took their places at the stove the moment any were vacated. The men surrounded it as though it was a saucy wench. They all crept up to embrace it.

"Down tools," they shouted. "Let's smoke."

They looked at one another to see who was going to light up. No one did. Either they had no tobacco or they were holding on to it, unwilling to let it be seen.

Shukhov went out with Pavlo. Gopchik loped behind like a hare.

"It's turned warmer," Shukhov said at once. "Eighteen, no lower. Fine for laying blocks."

They stole a glance at those blocks. The men had already thrown a lot of them up to the platform and a fair number had been shifted to the floor above.

Screwing up his eyes at the sun Shukhov checked its position. He was thinking of the captain's "decree".

Out in the open the wind was still having its way and the cold was still fierce. Don't forget, it was telling them, this is January.

The zeks' canteen was no more than a shanty made of boards nailed together round a stove, with some rusty metal strips over the cracks. Inside, it was partitioned into a kitchen and an eating-room. In neither was the floor boarded: it was pitted with the lumps and hollows that the men's feet had trodden into it. All that the kitchen consisted of was a square stove with a cauldron plastered into the top.

The kitchen was run by two men—a cook and a sanitary inspector. Every morning as he left the camp the cook drew an issue of groats from the main kitchen: about fifty grams a head, probably. That made one kilogram a team, a little less than a pood[1] for the whole column. The cook didn't fancy carrying the sack of groats all three kilometres himself, so he got a "helper" to carry it for him: better to give the "helper" an extra portion at the zeks' expense than burden his own back. There was water to be carried, too, and firewood for the stove, and these were jobs the cook didn't fancy either: so he found zeks to do them instead, for extra helpings at others' expense. What did it matter to him?

Then there was a rule that food must be eaten in the canteen; but the bowls couldn't be left there overnight, they'd have been filched by civilians, so about fifty, not more, had to be brought in, and quickly washed after use and turned over to the next diners (an extra helping for the man who carried the bowls). To make sure that no one took bowls from the canteen, a man must be posted at the door: but however vigilant he might be people took them all the same, either by distracting his attention or talking him round: so someone else had to go over the whole site, to collect dirty bowls and bring them back to the kitchen. And *he* got an extra helping. And many others got one too.

All the cook himself did was this: he poured the groats into the pot, adding salt; he divided the fat between the pot and himself (good fat didn't reach the zeks, and the rancid all went into the cauldron: so when there was an issue of rancid fat at the stores, the zeks welcomed it as an extra). Another thing he did: he stirred the kasha[2] when it was boiling.

The sanitary inspector had even less to do—he sat and watched: but when the porridge was ready he got his helping, as much as his belly would hold. And the cook too. Then the duty team-leader arrived—the team was changed every day—to have a taste and decide whether the stuff was good enough for the proles. He received a double portion.

The hooter sounded again. The team-leaders at once queued up, and the cook handed them bowls through the service-hatch. In the bottom of the bowls lay some porridge, how much you didn't ask, or try to judge by the weight. All you got if you opened your mouth was a good string of oaths.

The steppe was barren and windswept, with a dry wind in

[1] Sixteen kilograms.　　　　　　　　　　　　　[2] Porridge.

summer and a freezing one in winter. Nothing could ever grow in that steppe, less than nothing behind four barriers of barbed wire. Bread comes only from the bread-cutter, oats are threshed only in the store-house. And however much blood you sweat at work, however much you grovel on your belly, you'll force no food out of that earth; you'll get no more than the damned authorities give you. And you don't even get that—because of the cook and the "help" and all the other trusties in cushy jobs. They fleece you here, they fleece you in camp, they fleece you even earlier—in the stores. And those who do the fleecing don't swing picks. But you—you swing a pick and take what they give you. And get away from the serving hatch!

Pavlo and Shukhov, with Gopchik bringing up the rear, walked into the canteen. The men stood there so close to one another that you couldn't see either tables or benches. Some ate sitting down but most stood. The lads of the 82nd, who'd been pecking at those holes half a day without a chance of getting warm, had been the first to get in after the hooter: now even after they'd finished eating they didn't leave. Where else could they warm up? The oaths fell off them like water off a duck's back: it was so much more comfortable here than in the cold. Pavlo and Shukhov elbowed their way in. They'd arrived at a good moment: one team was being served, another was awaiting its turn, and there was only one deputy team-leader near the hatch. So, they were well ahead of the rest.

"Bowls, bowls," the cook shouted through the hatch and people hurriedly handed them over. Shukhov was collecting another lot and turning them in, not to get extra porridge but to get what was coming to him quicker.

Behind the partition some "helpers" were already washing bowls—for extra porridge.

The cook began to serve the deputy team-leaders who stood ahead of Pavlo in the queue.

"Gopchik," Pavlo shouted, over the heads of the men behind him.

"Here I am," came Gopchik's thin bleat from the door.

"Call the team."

Off he went.

The main thing today was that the porridge was good—

53

oatmeal porridge, the best sort. It wasn't often they had it. More often they got *magara* twice a day—a bran mash. But oatmeal is filling, it's good.

How often had Shukhov in his youth fed oats to horses! Never had it occurred to him that there'd come a time when his whole soul would crave for a handful of them.

"Bowls, bowls," shouted the cook.

Now the 104th was in the queue. That team-leader's deputy, up ahead, got his double helping and bounced away from the hatch.

This extra helping, too, was at the zeks' expense—but no one objected. The cook gave double helpings to all the team-leaders, and they either ate the extra helping themselves or gave it to their deputies. Tiurin gave his to Pavlo.

Shukhov's job now was to wedge himself in behind a table, oust two dawdlers, politely ask another prisoner to move, and clear a little space in front of him—for twelve bowls (to stand close together), with a second row of six, and two more on top. Next he had to take the bowls from Pavlo, repeating the number as he did so and keeping his eyes skinned—in case some outsider should nab a bowl from the table. And he had to see he wasn't jolted by someone's elbow so as to upset a bowl—right beside him people were leaving the table, stepping over the benches or squeezing in to eat. Yes, you had to keep your eyes skinned: was that fellow eating out of his own bowl? Or had he wormed his way up to one of the 104th's?

"Two, four, six," the cook counted at the hatch. He handed out the bowls two at a time—it was easier for him that way, otherwise he might count wrong.

"Two, four, six," Pavlo repeated quietly to himself, there at the hatch, in Ukrainian, and at once gave the bowls in pairs, to Shukhov, who put them on the table. Shukhov didn't repeat the numbers aloud—but he counted more sharply than anyone.

"Eight, ten."

Why wasn't Gopchik bringing in the team?

"Twelve, fourteen," the counting continued.

The kitchen ran out of bowls. Shukhov had a clear view through the hatch past Pavlo's head and shoulders. The cook put down two bowls on it and, keeping his hands on them, paused as

54

though thinking. Must be bawling out the dish-washers. But just then another lot of dirty bowls was pushed on to the hatch. The cook let go of the two clean ones he'd filled and pushed back the pile of dirty ones.

Shukhov left the fourteen bowls he'd already stacked on the table, straddled a bench, took the two filled ones from the hatch, and said quietly to Pavlo rather than to the cook:

"Fourteen."

"Stop! Where are you taking those bowls?" shouted the cook.

"He's from our team," Pavlo confirmed.

" 'Our team', but he's mixed up the count."

"Fourteen," Pavlo said with a shrug. Himself, he wouldn't have filched the extra bowls, for as deputy team-leader he had to maintain his dignity: but now he was simply repeating what Shukhov had said—he could always blame him for the mistake.

"I've already counted fourteen," the cook expostulated.

"So you did, but you didn't pass them out. You kept your hands on them," Shukhov shouted. "Come and count for yourself if you don't believe us. Look, they're all here on the table."

As he spoke he'd noticed the two Estonians pushing through to him, and he shoved the two bowls into their hands as they passed. And he'd managed to get back to the table to see that all the bowls were in place—the next tables hadn't pinched any, though they'd had ample opportunity to do so.

The cook's red face loomed large in the hatch.

"Where are those bowls?"he asked sternly.

"Here they are, at your service," yelled Shukhov. "Move along, scum, you're spoiling his view," he said to someone, giving him a shove. "Here they are, the pair of them." He picked up two bowls from the second row. "Here we have three rows of four, all nice and tidy. Count them."

"Hasn't your team come?" the cook asked, looking suspiciously round the small segment of the canteen he could see through the hatch—it had been kept narrow to prevent anyone looking into the kitchen and seeing how much was left in the cauldron.

"No, none of 'em are here yet," said Pavlo, shaking his head.

"Then why the hell are you taking bowls when the team's not here?"

"Here they come," yelled Shukhov.

And everyone heard the peremptory shouts of the captain at the door: "Why are you hanging on here?" he yelled, in his best quarter-deck voice. "If you've eaten, clear out and let others in."

The cook muttered something into the hatch. Then he drew himself up, and his hands could again be seen giving out the bowls: "Sixteen, eighteen."

Then he ladled the last portion, a double helping: "Twenty-three. That's all. Next team."

The men of the 104th pushed through. Pavlo handed them bowls passing them over the heads of the prisoners sitting at the second table.

In summer five could have sat on a bench, but now, as everyone was wearing thick clothes, four could barely fit in, and even they found it awkward to move their spoons.

Reckoning that of the two bowls of porridge that had been filched one at least would be his, Shukhov lost no time in applying himself to his first bowl. He drew his right knee up to his stomach, pulled his spoon ("Ust-Izhma, 1944") from under his boot-top, removed his hat, put it in his left armpit and ran his spoon round the edge of the kasha.

This is a moment that demands complete concentration, as you remove some of the scanty kasha from the bottom of the bowl, put it carefully into your mouth and shove it about there with your tongue. But Shukhov had to hurry, to show Pavlo he'd already finished and was waiting to be offered a second bowl. And there was Fetiukov to be reckoned with. He had come into the canteen with the two Estonians and had witnessed the whole affair of the two extra bowls. Now he stood there, straight in front of Pavlo, eyeing the four undistributed helpings as if to say that he ought to be given at least half a helping too.

Young swarthy Pavlo, however, went calmly on with his double portion, and there was no way of telling whether he noticed anyone standing there, or even remembered those extra bowls at all.

Shukhov finished his kasha. He had promised his belly two helpings, so one wasn't enough now to give him the full feeling he normally got from oatmeal kasha.

He groped in his inside pocket for the scrap of clean rag, found the unfrozen crescent of crust, and meticulously wiped off

56

with it the last remnant of mash from the bottom of the bowl and any that still clung to the brim. Then he licked the crust clean; then repeated the whole process. The bowl looked now as if it had been washed, with a dull film, nothing more, on the inside surface. He handed it over his shoulder to one of the dish-collectors and sat on, without replacing his hat.

Though it was Shukhov who had snaffled the extra bowls, it was for Pavlo to distribute them.

Pavlo prolonged the agony a little longer while emptying his own bowl. He didn't lick it clean; he merely gave a lick to his spoon, tucked it away and crossed himself. And then, very lightly, he touched—there wasn't room to move—two of the remaining four bowls. It meant he was giving them to Shukhov:

"Ivan Denisovich, take one for yourself and give the other to Tsezar."

Shukhov knew one of the bowls had to be taken to the office for Tsezar, who would never demean himself by going to the canteen or, for that matter, to the mess-hall in camp. He knew it, but, all the same, when Pavlo touched the bowls his heart contracted. Could Pavlo be giving him both? And now, as Pavlo spoke, his heart-beat went back to normal.

Without losing any time he leaned over his lawful spoil and began to eat with deliberation, insensitive to the thumps on his back that the zeks in the next team were dealing him. The only thing that vexed him was that the second bowl might still go to Fetuikov. Fetuikov was a past-master at cadging, but he lacked the courage to swipe anything.

Nearby sat Captain Buinovsky. He had long finished his kasha. He didn't know the team had two extra portions to dispose of. He didn't look about to see how much Pavlo still had left to hand out. He was simply relaxing, warming up. He was not strong enough to rise to his feet and go out into the cold or into that frigid warming-up point. He, like the very people he had just hounded out of the canteen with his rasping voice, was occupying a place he had no right to and getting in the way of the next team. He was a newcomer. He was unused to the hard life of the zeks. Though he didn't know it, moments like this were particularly important to him, for they were transforming him from an eager, confident naval officer with a ringing voice into an inert, though wary, zek. And only in that inertness lay the chance of surviving the twenty-five years of imprisonment he'd been sentenced to.

People were already shouting at him and jogging him in the back to make him give up his place.

"Captain!" said Pavlo. "Hey, captain."

Buinovsky shuddered as though he was being jerked out of a dream. He looked round.

Pavlo handed him a bowl of kasha. He didn't ask him whether he wanted it.

The captain's eyebrows shot up. He looked at the bowl as at something miraculous.

"Take it, take it," said Pavlo reassuringly, and picking up the last bowl—for the team-leader—went out.

An apologetic smile flitted over the captain's chapped lips. And this man, who had sailed round Europe and navigated the Great Northern Route, leaned happily over half a ladleful of thin oatmeal kasha, cooked entirely without fat—just oats and water.

Fetiukov cast angry looks at Shukhov and the captain and left the canteen.

But Shukhov thought Pavlo had been right. In time the captain would learn the ropes. Meanwhile, he didn't know how to live.

Shukhov still nursed a faint hope that Tsezar would give him his bowl of kasha. But it seemed unlikely, for more than a fortnight had passed since Tsezar had received his last parcel.

After scraping the bottom and rim of the second bowl in the same way as the first, then licking the crust, Shukhov finally ate the crust itself. Then he picked up Tsezar's bowl of cold kasha and went out.

"It's for the office," he said, as he pushed past the man on the door who tried to stop him taking the bowl out.

The office was in a log cabin near the sentry-house. As in the morning, smoke was curling out of the chimney. The stove was kept going by an orderly who worked as an errand boy too, picking up a few copecks here and there. They didn't grudge him chips or even logs for the office-stove.

The outer door creaked as Shukhov opened it. Then came another door, caulked with oakum. Bringing with him a cloud of frosty vapour he went in and quickly pulled the door to (so that they wouldn't yell at him: "Hey, you lout, shut the door").

The office was as hot as a bath-house, it seemed to Shukhov. The sun, coming in through the icy window-panes, played gaily in the room, not angrily as it did at the power-station; and, spreading across the broad sunbeam, the smoke of Tsezar's pipe looked like incense in church. The stove glowed red right through. How they piled it on, the devils! Even the stove-pipe was red-hot.

In such a fug you've only to sit down a minute and you're off to sleep on the spot.

The office had two rooms. The door into the second one, occupied by the superintendent, was not quite closed, and through it the superintendent's voice was thundering:

"There's an overdraft on the expenses for labour and building materials. Right under your noses prisoners are chopping up valuable planks, not to mention prefabricated panels, and using them for firewood at their warming-up points. The other day the prisoners unloaded cement near the stores in a high wind. What's more, they carried it for up to ten paces on barrows. As a result the whole area round the store is ankle-deep in cement and the men are smothered in it. Imagine the loss!"

Obviously a conference was going on in there. With the foremen.

In a corner near the door an orderly sat lazing on a stool. Beyond him, like a bent pole, stooped Shkuropatenko—B 219. That eyesore—staring out of the window, trying to see, even now, whether anyone was pinching some of his precious prefabs! You didn't spot us *that* time, you gawk!

The book-keepers, also zeks, were toasting bread at the stove. To prevent it from burning they'd contrived a grill out of wire.

Tsezar was sprawling over his desk, smoking a pipe. His back was to Shukhov and he didn't notice him come in.

Opposite him sat X 123, a stringy old man who was serving a twenty-year sentence. He was eating kasha.

"No, my dear fellow," Tsezar was saying in a gentle, casual way. "If one is to be objective one must acknowledge that Eisenstein is a genius. *Ivan the Terrible*, isn't that a work of genius? The dance of the masked *oprichniki*! The scene in the cathedral!"

"Ham," said X 123 angrily, arresting his spoon before his lips. "It's all so arty there's no art left in it. Spice and poppy-seed instead of everyday bread and butter! And then, that vile political idea—the justification of personal tyranny. A mockery of the memory of three generations of Russian intelligentsia."

He ate as if his lips were made of wood. The kasha would do him no good.

"But what other interpretation would have been allowed?"

"Allowed? Ugh! Then don't call him a genius! Call him an arse-licker, obeying a vile dog's order. Geniuses don't adjust their interpretations to suit the taste of tyrants!"

"Hm, hm!" Shukhov cleared his throat. He hadn't the nerve to interrupt such a learned conversation. But there wasn't any sense standing there, either.

Tsezar swung round and held out his hand for the bowl, not even looking at Shukhov, as though the kasha had materialised out of thin air.

"But listen," he resumed. "Art isn't a matter of *what* but of *how*."

X 123 struck the table angrily with the edge of his hand.

"To bloody hell with your 'how' if it doesn't arouse any good feelings in me."

Shukhov stood there just as long as was decent for a man who had brought a bowl of kasha. After all, Tsezar might offer him a smoke. But Tsezar had quite forgotten his presence.

So Shukhov turned on his heel and went quietly out. The cold was bearable, he decided. The block-laying wouldn't go too badly.

As he walked along the path he caught sight in the snow of a short length of steel—a bit of a hacksaw-blade.

He could conceive of no immediate use for it, but then you can never tell what you might need in the future. So he picked it up and slipped it into his knee-pocket. He'd hide it at the power-station. Thrift was better than riches.

The first thing he did on reaching the power-station was to take his trowel out of its hiding-place and slip it under the length of cord he wore round his waist. Then he made a dive for the machine-shop.

After the sunlight the shop seemed quite dark and no warmer than outside. Sort of clammy.

All the men had crowded about the round iron stove that Shukhov had fixed, or near the one where the sand was steaming as it dried. Those who could find no room round the stoves sat on the edge of the mortar-box. Tiurin was seated against the stove, finishing the kasha that Pavlo had warmed up for him on it. The lads were whispering to one another. They were in high spirits. One of them passed the news on to Shukhov: the team-leader had been successful in fixing the work-report. He'd come back in a good mood.

What sort of work he'd found and how it had been rated was Tiurin's own business. What in fact had the team done that first half of the day? Not a thing. They weren't paid for fixing the stoves, they weren't paid for arranging a place to warm up in: they had done that for themselves, not for the building-site. But something had to be written in the report. Perhaps Tsezar was helping the team-leader to fix it up properly. It wasn't for nothing that Tiurin treated him with respect. A cleverly fixed work-report meant good rations for five days. Well, say four: out of the five the authorities would wangle one for themselves by putting the whole camp on to the guaranteed minimum—the same for all, the best and the worst. Seems to be fair enough: equal rations for all. But it's an economy at the expense of our bellies. Well, a zek's belly can stand anything. Scrape through today somehow and hope for tomorrow.

This was the hope they all had to go to sleep with when they got only the guaranteed minimum.

But when you thought about it, it was five days' work for four days' food.

The shop was quiet. Zeks who had tobacco were smoking. The light was dim, and the men sat gazing into the fire. Like a big family. It was a family, the team. They were listening to Tiurin as he talked to two or three of the men by the stove. Tiurin never wasted his words, and if he permitted himself to talk then he was in a good humour.

He too hadn't learned to eat with his hat on, and when his head was bared he looked old. He was close-cropped like all of them, but in the light of the flames you could see how many white hairs he had.

"I'd be shaking in my boots before a battalion commander and here was the regimental commander himself. 'Red Army man Tiurin at your service,' I reported. The commander looked at me hard from under a pair of fierce eyebrows as he asked me my full name. I told him. Year of birth. I told him. It was in the 'thirties and I was, let's see, just twenty-two then, just a calf. 'Well, Tiurin, how are you serving?' 'I serve the working people.' I replied, with a salute. He flared up and banged both fists on the desk, wham! 'You're serving the working people, you scum, but what are you yourself?' I went cold inside but I kept a grip on myself. 'Machine-gunner, first-class. Excellent marks in military training and polit. . . .' 'First class! What are you talking about, you rat? Your father's a kulak. Look, this document has come from Kamen. Your father's a kulak and you've been hiding. They've been looking for you for two years.' I turned pale and held my tongue. I hadn't written a line home for a year, to prevent them from tracing me. And how they were living at home I'd no idea. And they knew nothing about me. 'Where's your conscience?' he shouted at me, all four bars on his collar shaking. 'Aren't you ashamed of yourself for deceiving the Soviet Power?' I thought he was going to strike me. But he didn't. He wrote out an order. To have me thrown out of the army at six o'clock that very day. It was November. They stripped me of my winter uniform and issued me with a summer one, a third-hand one it must've been, and a short, tight greatcoat. I didn't know at the time that I needn't have given my winter uniform up, just sent them to . . . So they packed me off with that slip of paper: 'Discharged from the ranks . . . as a kulak's son.' A fine reference for getting a job! I had a four-day train journey ahead of me to get home. They didn't give me a free pass, they didn't provide me with even one day's rations. Just gave me dinner for the last time and threw me out of the cantonment.

'Incidentally, in 'thirty-eight, at the Kotlas deportation point, I met my former platoon commander. He'd been given ten years too. I learned from him that the regimental commander and the commissar were both shot in 'thirty-seven, no matter whether they were proletarian or kulak stock, whether they had a conscience or not. So I crossed myself and said: 'So, after all, Creator, You do exist up there in heaven. Your patience is long-suffering but You strike hard.' "

After two bowls of kasha Shukhov so longed to smoke he felt he'd die if he didn't. And, reckoning he could buy those two

62

glassfuls of cottage-grown tobacco from the Lett in Hut 7, he said in a low voice to the Estonian fisherman:

"Listen, Eino, lend me some for a cigarette till tomorrow. You know I won't let you down."

Eino gave him a hard look and then slowly turned his eyes to his "brother". They shared everything: one of them wouldn't spend even a pinch of tobacco without consulting the other. They muttered something together and Eino reached for his pink-embroidered pouch. Out of it he extracted a pinch of tobacco, factory-cut, placed it in Shukhov's palm, measured it with his eye and added a few more strands. Just enough for one cigarette, no more.

Shukhov had a piece of newspaper ready. He tore off a scrap, rolled the cigarette, picked up a glowing coal from where it lay at Tiurin's feet—and drew and drew. A sweet dizziness went all through his body, to his head, to his feet, as if he had downed a glass of vodka.

The moment he began to smoke he felt, blazing at him from across the length of the shop, a pair of green eyes—Fetiukov's. He might have relented and given him a drag, the jackal, but he'd seen him pulling off one of his sponges already that day. No: better leave something for Senka instead. Senka hadn't heard the team-leader's tale and sat in front of the fire, poor wretch, his head on one side.

Tiurin's pock-marked face was lit up by the flames. He spoke calmly, as if he were telling someone else's story:

"What rags I had, I sold for a quarter of their value. I bought a couple of loaves from under the counter—they'd already started bread-rationing. I'd thought of hopping on to a goods-train, but they'd just introduced some stiff penalties for that. And, if you remember, you couldn't buy tickets even if you had the money; you had to produce special little books or show travel-documents. There was no getting on to the platform either—militia men at the barrier, and guards wandering about the lines at both ends of the station. It was a cold sunset and the puddles were freezing over. Where was I going to spend the night? I straddled a brick wall, jumped over with my two loaves and slipped into the platform lavatory. I waited in there for a while. No one was after me. I came out as though I were a soldier-passenger. The Vladivostok-

Moscow was standing in the station. There was a crowd round the hot-water tap, people banging each other's heads with their kettles. On the edge of the crowd I noticed a girl in a blue jersey— her kettle was a big one. She was scared of pushing through to the tap. Didn't want her little feet trodden on or scalded. 'Look,' I said to her, 'hang on to these loaves and I'll fill your kettle in a jiffy.' While I was doing so off jerked the train. She was holding the loaves. She burst into tears. What was she to do with them? She didn't mind losing the kettle. 'Run,' I called to her, 'I'll follow you.' Off she went, with me on her heels. I caught her up and hoisted her on the train with one arm. The train was going quite fast. I had a foot on it too. The conductor didn't slash at my fingers or shove me in the chest—there were other soldiers in the carriage and he took me for one of them."

Shukhov nudged Senka in the ribs: come on, finish this, you poor sod. He handed him the cigarette in his wooden holder. Let him suck on it, he's all right. Senka, the chump, accepted it like an actor, pressed one hand to his heart and bowed his head. But, after all, he was deaf.

Tiurin went on:

"There were six, all girls, in a compartment to themselves— Leningrad students travelling back from technical courses. A lovely spread on their little table; mackintoshes swinging from coat-hangers; posh suitcases. They were going through life happily. All clear ahead for them. We talked and joked and drank tea together.

"They asked me what coach I was in. I sighed and told them the truth. 'I'm in a special coach, girls, heading straight for death.' "

There was silence in the shop. All you could hear was the stove roaring.

"Well, they gasped and moaned and put their heads together. And the result was they covered me with their mackintoshes on the top berth. They hid me all the way to Novosibirsk. By the way, I was able to show my gratitude to one of them later: she was swept up by the Kirov wave in 'thirty-five. She was just about done in, working in a hard-labour team, and I got her fixed up in the tailoring shop."

"Shall we mix the mortar?" Pavlo asked Tiurin in a whisper.

Tiurin didn't hear him.

"I came up to our house at night, through the back garden. I left the same night. I took my little brother with me, went off with him to warmer parts, to Frunze. I'd nothing to give him to eat, and nothing for myself either. In Frunze some road-workers were boiling asphalt in a pot, with all kinds of riff-raff and waifs sitting round. I sat down among them and said: 'Hey, you gents, take on my little brother as a learner. Teach him how to live.' They took him. I'm only sorry I didn't join the crooks myself."

"And you never saw your brother again?" asked the captain.

Tiurin yawned.

"Never again."

He yawned once more.

"Well, don't mope, lads," he said. "We'll live through it, even in this power-station. Get going, the mortar-mixers. Don't wait for the hooter."

That's what a team is. A guard can't get people to budge even in working hours, but a team-leader can tell his men to get on with the job even during the break, and they'll do it. Because he's the one who feeds them. And he'd never make them work for nothing.

If they were going to start mixing the mortar only when the hooter went, then the masons would have to hang about waiting for it.

Shukhov drew a deep breath and got to his feet.

"I'll go up and chip the ice off."

He took with him a small hatchet and a brush and, for the laying, a mason's hammer, a levelling-staff, a plumb and a length of string.

Kilgas looked at him, a wry expression on his ruddy-cheeked face. Why should *he* jump up before his team-leader told him to? But after all, thought Shukhov, Kilgas didn't have to worry about feeding the team. All the same to him, the bald head, if he got a couple of hundred grams less—he'd manage on his parcels.

Still, he stirred himself, did Kilgas: you can't keep the team waiting, he understood, just because of *you*.

"Wait a tick, Vanya, I'm coming too," he said.

"There you are, fat-face. If you'd been working for yourself you'd have been on your feet in a jiffy."

65

(There was another reason why Shukhov hurried: he wanted to lay his hands on that plumb before Kilgas. They'd drawn only one from the tool store.)

"Sure three are enough for the block-laying?" Pavlo asked Tiurin. "Shouldn't we send another man up? Or won't there be enough mortar?"

Tiurin knitted his brows and thought.

"I'll make the fourth myself, Pavlo. You work here on the mortar. It's a big box, we'll put six on the job. Work like this: take the mortar out from one end when it's ready and use the other for mixing some more. And see there's a steady flow. Not a moment's break."

"Ekh!" Pavlo sprang to his feet. He was young, his blood was fresh, camp life hadn't as yet worn him out. His face had been fattened on Ukrainian dumplings. "If *you're* going to lay blocks, I'll make the mortar for you myself. We'll see who's working the harder. Hey, where's the longest spade?"

That's what a team-leader is too. Pavlo had been a forest sniper, he'd even been on night raids. Try and make *him* break his back in a camp! But to work for the team-leader—that was different.

Shukhov and Kilgas came out on to the second storey. They heard Senka creaking up the ramp behind them. So he'd guessed, the deaf'un.

Only a start had been made with laying the blocks on the second-storey walls. Three rows all round, a bit higher here and there. That was when the laying went fastest. From the knee to the chest, without the help of a platform.

All the platforms and trestles that had been there had been pilfered by the zeks: some had been carried off to other buildings, some had been burned. Anything to prevent another team getting them. But now everything had to be done in good order. To-morrow they must nail some trestles together, otherwise the work would be held up.

You could see a long way from up there: the whole snow-clad, deserted expanse of the site (the zeks were hiding away, warming up before the dinner-break ended), the dark watch-towers and the sharp-tipped poles for the barbed-wire. You couldn't see the wire itself except when you looked into the sun. The sun was very bright, it made you blink.

And also, not far away, you could see the mobile electro-station smoking away, blackening the sky. And wheezing, too. It always made that hoarse, sickly noise before it hooted. There it went. So they hadn't, after all, cut too much off the dinner-break.

"Hey, stakhanovite! Hurry up with that plumb," Kilgas shouted.

"Look how much ice you've got left on your wall! See if you can manage to chip it off before evening," Shukhov said derisively. "*You* needn't have brought your trowel up with you!"

They'd intended to start with the walls they'd been allocated before dinner, but Tiurin called from below:

"Hey, lads! We'll work in pairs, so that the mortar doesn't freeze in the hods. You take Senka with you on your wall, and I'll work with Kilgas. But to start with, you stand in for me, Gopchik, and clean up Kilgas's wall."

Shukhov and Kilgas looked at one another. Correct. Quicker that way.

They grabbed their axes.

And now Shukhov was no longer seeing that distant view where the sun gleamed on snow. He was no longer seeing the prisoners as they wandered from the warming-up places all over the site, some to hack away at the pits they hadn't finished that morning, some to fix the mesh reinforcement, some to erect trusses in the work-shops. Shukhov was seeing only his wall—from the junction where the blocks rose in steps, higher than his waist, to where it met Kilgas's. He showed Senka where to remove ice and chopped at it zealously himself with the back and blade of his axe, so that splinters of ice flew all about and into his face. He worked with zest, but his thoughts were elsewhere. His thoughts and his eyes were feeling their way under the ice to the wall itself, the outer façade of the power station, two blocks thick. At the spot he was working on, the wall had previously been laid by some mason who was either incompetent or had scamped the job. But now Shukhov tackled the wall as if it was his own handiwork. There, he saw, was a cavity that couldn't be levelled up in one row: he'd have to do it in three, adding a little more mortar each time. And here the outer wall bellied a bit—it would take two rows to straighten that. He divided the wall mentally into the place where

67

he would lay blocks, starting at the point where they rose in steps, and the place where Senka was working, on the right, up to Kilgas's section. There in the corner, he reckoned, Kilgas wouldn't hold back, he would lay a few blocks for Senka, to make things easier for him. And, while they were pottering about in the corner, Shukhov would forge ahead and have half the wall built, so that his pair wouldn't be behindhand. He noted how many blocks he'd require for each of the places. And the moment the carriers brought the blocks up he shouted at Alyosha:

"Bring 'em to me. Put 'em here. And here."

Senka had finished chipping off the ice, and Shukhov picked up a wire brush, gripped it in both hands, and went along the wall swishing it—to and fro, to and fro—cleaning up the top row, especially the joints, till only a snowy film was left on it.

Tiurin climbed up and, while Shukhov was still busy with his brush, fixed up a levelling-rod in the corner. Shukhov and Kilgas had already placed theirs on the edges of their walls.

"Hey," called Pavlo from below. "Anyone alive up there? Take the mortar."

Shukhov broke into a sweat: he hadn't stretched his string over the blocks yet. He was hard pressed. He decided to stretch it for three rows at once, and make the necessary allowance. He decided also to take over a little of the outer wall from Senka and give him some of the inside instead: things would be easier for him that way.

Stretching his string along the top edge, he explained to Senka, with mouthings and gestures, where he was to work. Senka understood, for all his deafness. He bit his lips and glanced aside with a nod at Tiurin's wall. "Shall we make it hot for him?" his look said. We shan't trail behind. He laughed.

Now the mortar was being brought up the ramp. Tiurin decided not to have any of it dumped beside the masons—it would only freeze while being shifted on to the hods. The men were to put down their barrows: the masons would take the mortar straight from them and get on with the laying. Meanwhile the carriers, not to waste time, would shift on the blocks that other prisoners were heaving up from below. Directly the mortar had been scooped up from one pair of barrows, another pair would be coming and the first would go down. At the stove in the mortar-shop, the

68

carriers would thaw out any mortar that had frozen to their barrows—and themselves too, while they were at it.

The barrows came up two at a time—one for Kilgas's wall, one for Shukhov's. The mortar steamed in the frost but held no real warmth in it. You slapped it on the wall with your trowel and if you dawdled it would freeze: and then you'd have to hit it with the side of a hammer—you couldn't scrape it off with a trowel. And if you laid a block a bit out of true, it would immediately freeze too and set crooked: then you'd need the back of your axe to knock it off and chip away the mortar.

But Shukhov made no mistakes. The blocks varied. If any had chipped corners or broken edges or lumps on their sides, he noticed it at once and saw which way up to lay them and where they would fit best on the wall.

Here was one. Shukhov took up some of the steaming mortar on his trowel and chucked it into the appropriate place, with his mind on the joint below (this would have to be just at the middle of the block he was going to lay). He chucked on just enough mortar to go under the one block. Then he snatched it from the pile—carefully, though, so as not to tear his mittens, for with blocks you can do that in no time. He smoothed the mortar with his trowel and then—down with the block! And without losing a moment he levelled it, patting it with the side of the trowel—it wasn't lying quite trim—so that the wall should be truly in line and the block lie level both lengthwise and across. The mortar was already freezing.

Now if some mortar had oozed out to the side, you had to chop it off as quickly as possible with the edge of your trowel and fling it over the wall (in summer it would go under the next brick, but now it was impossible). Next you took another look at the joint below, for there were times when the block had partially crumbled. In that event, you slapped in some extra mortar where the defect was, and you didn't lay the block flat—you slid it from side to side, squeezing out the extra mortar between it and its neighbour. An eye on the plumb. An eye on the surface. Set. Next.

The work went with a swing. Once two rows were laid and the old faults levelled up it would go quite smoothly. But now was the time to keep your eyes skinned.

Shukhov forged ahead; he pressed along the outside wall to

meet Senka. Senka had parted with Tiurin in the corner and was now working along the wall to meet him.

Shukhov winked at the mortar-carriers. Bring it up, bring it up. Steady now. Smart's the word. He was working so fast he hadn't time to wipe his nose.

He and Senka met and began to scoop out of the same mortar-hod. It didn't take them long to scrape it to the bottom.

"Mortar!" Shukhov shouted over the wall.

"Coming up!" shouted Pavlo.

Another load arrived. They emptied that one too—all the liquid mortar in it, anyhow. The rest had already frozen to the sides. Scrape it off yourselves! If you don't it's you who'll be taking it up and down again. Off you go! Next!

And now Shukhov and the other masons felt the cold no longer. Thanks to the urgent work, the first wave of heat had come over them—when you feel wet under your coat, under your jacket, under your shirt and your vest. But they didn't stop for a moment: they hurried on with the laying. And after about an hour they had their second flush of heat, the one that dries up the sweat. Their feet didn't feel cold, that was the main thing. Nothing else mattered. Even the breeze, light but piercing, couldn't distract them from the work. Only Senka stamped his feet—he had enormous ones, poor sod, and they'd given him a pair of valenki too tight for him.

From time to time Tiurin would shout "Mo-o-rtar," and Shukhov would shout "Mo-o-rtar"—he was shouting to his own men. When you're working all out, you're a sort of team-leader to your neighbours yourself. It was for Shukhov to keep up with the other pair: now, he'd have made his own brother sweat up with the mortar.

At first, after dinner, Buinovsky had carried mortar with Fetiukov. But the ramp was steep and dangerous, and the captain dragged his feet to begin with. Shukhov urged him on gently:

"Quicker, captain. Blocks, captain."

Every time Buinovsky came up he worked more briskly. Fetiukov, on the other hand, grew lazier and lazier. He'd tilt the barrow as he came up, the bitch's twat, so that the mortar would slop out of it and then it'd be lighter to carry.

Shukhov poked him in the back:

"Ugh, you bloody rat. I'll wager you made your men sweat all right, when you were an overseer."

Buinovsky appealed to the team-leader:

"Give me a man to work with. I won't go on working with this shit."

Tiurin agreed. He sent Fetiukov to heave up blocks from below; and made him work, on top of that, where the number of blocks he handled was counted separately. He told Alyosha to work with the captain. Alyosha was a quiet lad, anyone could order him about.

"It's all hands on deck, middy," the captain urged. "See how fast they're laying blocks?"

Alyosha smiled meekly:

"If it's necessary to work faster then let's work faster. Just as you say."

And tramped down for the next load.

What a treasure's a meek man for a team!

Tiurin shouted to someone down below. Another lorry-load of blocks had apparently arrived. Not one had been brought here for six months; now they were pouring in. You could work really fast as long as the lorries brought blocks. But this wouldn't go on. Later there'd be a hold-up in the delivery and then you'd stand idle yourself.

Tiurin was bawling out to someone else down below. Something about the hoist. Shukhov would have liked to know what was up but he'd no time to find out: he was levelling his wall. The carriers came up and told him: a fitter had come to repair the motor of the hoist, and the superintendent of electrical repairs, a civilian, was with him. The fitter was tinkering with the motor, the superintendent watched.

That was according to the rules: one man works, one man watches.

Good if they repaired the hoist now. It could be used for both blocks and mortar.

Shukhov was laying his third row (Kilgas too was on his third), when up the ramp came yet another snooper, another chief—building-foreman Der. A Muscovite. Used to work in some ministry, it was said.

Shukhov was standing close to Kilgas, and drew his attention to Der.

"Ugh!" said Kilgas contemptuously. "I don't deal with the big shots generally. But you can call me if he slips off the ramp."

And now Der took up his stand behind the masons and watched them work. Shukhov hated these snoopers like poison. Trying to make himself into an engineer, the pig's snout! Once he'd shown Shukhov how to lay bricks—and given him a belly laugh. A man should build a house with his own hands before he calls himself an engineer.

At Shukhov's village of Temgenovo there were no brick houses. All the cottages were timber-built. The school too was a wooden building, made from six-foot logs. But the camp needed masons and Shukhov, glad to oblige, became a mason. A man with two trades to his credit can easily learn another ten.

No, Der didn't fall off the ramp, though once he stumbled. He came up almost at the double.

"Tiu-u-urin," he shouted, his eyes popping out of his head. "Tiu-u-urin."

At his heels came Pavlo. He was carrying the spade he'd been working with.

Der was wearing a regulation camp-coat but it was new and clean. His hat was stylish, made of leather, though, like everyone else's, it bore a number—B 731.

"Well?" Tiurin went up to him trowel in hand, his hat tilted over one eye.

Something out of the ordinary was brewing. Something not to be missed. Yet the mortar was growing cold in the barrows. Shukhov went on working—working and listening.

"What d'you think you're doing?" Der spluttered. "This isn't a matter of the lock-up. This is a criminal offence, Tiurin. You'll get a third term for this."

Only then did Shukhov catch on to what was up. He glanced at Kilgas. He'd understood, too. The roofing-felt. Der had spotted it on the windows.

Shukhov feared nothing for himself. His team-leader would never give him away. He was afraid for Tiurin. To the team Tiurin was a father, for *them* he was a pawn. Up in the North they readily gave team-leaders a second term for a thing like this.

Ugh, what a mug Tiurin pulled. He flung down that trowel of

his and took a pace towards Der. Der looked round. Pavlo lifted his spade.

He hadn't grabbed it for nothing.

And Senka, for all his deafness, had understood. He came up, hands on hips. And Senka was a hefty bloke.

Der blinked, gave a sort of twitch, and looked round for a way of escape.

Tiurin leaned up against him and said quite softly, though distinctly enough for everyone to hear:

"Your time for giving terms has passed, you rat. If you say a word, you blood-sucker, this is your last day on earth. Remember that."

Tiurin shook, shook uncontrollably.

Hatchet-faced Pavlo looked Der straight in the eyes. A look as sharp as a razor.

"Steady now, lads, steady." Der turned pale and edged away from the ramp.

Without another word Tiurin straightened his hat, picked up his trowel and walked back to his wall.

Pavlo, very slowly, went down the ramp with his spade.

Slo-o-owly.

Der was as scared to stay as to leave. He took shelter behind Kilgas and stood there.

Kilgas went on laying blocks, the way they hand out medicine at a chemist's—like a doctor, measuring everything so carefully— his back to Der, as if he didn't even know he was there.

Der stole up to Tiurin. Where was all his arrogance?

"But what shall I tell the superintendent, Tiurin?"

Tiurin went on working. He said, without turning his head:

"You will tell him it was like that when we arrived. We came and that's how it was."

Der waited a little longer. They weren't going to bump him off now, he saw. He took a few steps and put his hands in his pockets.

"Hey, S 854," he muttered. "Why are you using such a thin layer of mortar?"

He had to get his own back at someone's expense. He couldn't find fault with Shukhov for his joints or for the straightness of his line, so he decided he was laying the mortar too thin.

73

"Permit me to point out," Shukhov lisped derisively, "that if the mortar is laid on thick in weather like this the place will be like a sieve in the spring."

"You're a mason. Listen to what a foreman has to tell you," Der said with a frown, puffing out his cheeks in that way of his.

Well, here and there it might be a bit on the thin side. He could have used a little more—but only, after all, if he'd been laying the blocks in decent conditions, not in winter. The man ought to have a heart. You've got to show some output. But what was the good of trying to explain? He didn't want to understand.

Der went quietly down the ramp.

"You get me that hoist repaired," Tiurin sang out after him. "What d'you think we are—donkeys? Carrying blocks up to the second storey by hand."

"They'll pay you for taking them up," Der called back from the ramp, quite humbly.

"At the wheelbarrow rate? Child's play to push up a wheelbarrow. We've got to be paid for carrying them up by hand."

"Don't think I'm against it. But the book-keepers won't consent to the higher rate."

"The book-keepers! I've got a whole team sweating to keep those four masons at work. How much d'you think we'll earn?" Tiurin shouted, pressing on without a break.

"Mort-o-ar," he called down.

"Mort-o-ar," echoed Shukhov. They'd levelled off the whole of the third row. On the fourth they'd really get going. Time to stretch the string for the next row, but he could manage this way too.

Der went off across the open ground, looking haggard. To warm up in the office. He must have had the wind up. But he should have thought a bit before taking on a wolf like Tiurin. He should keep pleasant with team-leaders like that, then he'd have nothing to worry about: the camp authorities didn't insist on his doing any real hard work, he received top-category rations, he lived in a separate cabin—what else did he want? Giving himself airs, trying to be smart.

The lads coming up with the mortar said the fitter and superintendent had left. The mortar was past repair.

Very well, haul 'em up by hand.

For as long as Shukhov had worked with machinery the machines had either broken down or been smashed by the zeks. He'd seen them wreck a log-conveyer by shoving a beam under the chain and leaning hard on it, to give themselves a breather; they were stacking log by log with never a moment to stretch their backs.

"Damn the whole —— lot of you!" shouted Tiurin, warming up.

"Pavlo's asking how you're getting on for mortar," someone called from below.

"Mix some more."

"We've got half a box mixed."

"Mix another."

What a pace they set! They were driving along the fifth row now. They'd had to double themselves up when they were working on the first row, but now the wall had risen shoulder-high. And why shouldn't they race on?—there were no windows or doors to allow for, just a couple of adjoining blank walls and plenty of blocks. Shukhov should have stretched a string higher but there was no time for it.

"The eighty-second have gone off to hand in their tools," Gopchik reported.

Tiurin looked at him witheringly.

"Mind your own business, you shrimp. Bring some blocks."

Shukhov looked about. Yes, the sun was beginning to set. It had a greyish appearance as it sank in a red haze. And they'd got into the swing—couldn't be better. They'd started on the fifth row now. Ought to finish it today. Level it off.

The mortar-carriers were snorting like winded horses. Buinovsky was quite grey in the face. He might not be forty but he wasn't far off it.

The cold was growing keener. Busy as were Shukhov's hands, the frost nipped his fingers through the shabby mittens. And it was piercing his left boot too. He stamped his foot. Thud, thud.

By now he needn't stoop to the wall, but he still had to bend his aching back for each block and each scoop of mortar.

"Hey, boys!" he pestered the men handling the blocks. "You'd better put them on the wall for me. Heave 'em up here."

75

The captain would gladly have obliged but lacked the strength. He wasn't used to the work. But Alyosha said:

"All right, Ivan Denisovich. Show me where to put them."

You could count on Alyosha. Did whatever was asked of him. If everybody in the world was like that, Shukhov would have done likewise. If a man asks for help why not help him? Those Baptists had got something there.

The rail clanged. The signal went dinning all over the site and reached the power-station. They'd been caught with some unused mortar. Ekh, just when they'd got into the swing of it!

"Mortar! Mortar!" Tiurin shouted.

A new boxful had only just been mixed. They had to go on laying, there was no other way. If they left anything in the box, next morning they could throw the whole lot of it to hell—the mortar would have petrified, it wouldn't yield to a pickaxe.

"Don't let me down, brothers," Shukhov shouted.

Kilgas was fuming. He didn't like speed-ups. But he pressed on all the same. What else could he do?

Pavlo ran up with a barrow, a trowel in his belt, and began laying himself. Five trowels on the job now.

Now look out for where the rows meet. Shukhov visualized what shape of block was needed there, and shoving a hammer into Aloysha's hand egged him on:

"Knock a bit off this one."

Hasty work is scamped work. Now that all of them were racing one another Shukhov bided his time, keeping an eye on the wall. He pushed Senka to the left and took over the laying himself towards the main corner on the right. It would be a disaster if the walls overlapped or if the corner shouldn't be level. Cost them half a day's work tomorrow.

"Stop!" He shoved Pavlo away from a block and levelled it himself. And from his place in the corner he noticed that Senka's section was sagging. He hurried over to Senka and levelled it out with two blocks.

The captain brought up a load of mortar, enough for a good horse.

"Another two barrowsful," he said.

The captain was tottering. But he went on sweating away. Shukhov had had a horse like that once. He'd cherished it

76

but then they'd driven it to death. They'd stripped the hide off it.

The top rim of the sun dipped below the horizon. Now without Gopchik having to tell them they saw that the teams had not only turned in their tools but were pouring up to the gates. No one came out into the open immediately after the signal, only a fool would go and freeze out there. They sat in the warmth. But the moment came, by agreement between the team-leaders, when all the teams poured out together. Without this agreement, the zeks, a stubborn lot, would have sat each other out in the warmth till midnight.

Tiurin himself realized that he'd cut things too fine. The man in charge of the tool-store must be showering a dozen oaths on him.

"Ekh," he shouted, "don't spare the shit! Carriers! Go and scrape the big box, and out with what's left into that hole there and scatter some snow on it to keep it hidden. You, Pavlo, take a couple of men, collect the tools and hand them in. I'll send Gopchik after you with the three trowels. We'll use up the last two loads of mortar before we knock off."

Everyone dashed to his job. They took Shukhov's hammer from him and wound up his string. The mortar-carriers and the block-lifters hurried down into the mortar-shop. They'd nothing more to do up there. Three masons remained on top, Kilgas, Senka and Shukhov. Tiurin walked about to see how much wall they'd built. He was pleased. "Not bad, eh? In half a day. Without any —— hoist."

Shukhov noticed there was a little mortar left in Kilgas's hod. He didn't want to waste it, but was worried that the team-leader might be reprimanded if the trowels were handed in late.

"Listen, lads," he said, "give your trowels to Gopchik. Mine's not on the list. There's no need to hand it in. I'll keep going."

Tiurin said with a laugh:

"How can we ever let you out? We just can't spare you."

Shukhov laughed too, and went on working.

Kilgas took the trowels, Senka went on handing blocks to Shukhov. They poured Kilgas's mortar into Shukhov's hod.

Gopchik ran across to the tool-store, to overtake Pavlo. The rest were as anxious to be in time, and hurried over to the gates, without Tiurin. A team-leader is a power, but the escort is a greater power still. They list late-comers, and that means the cells for you.

There was a terrible crowd near the gates now. Everyone had collected there. It looked as if the escort had come out and started counting.

(They counted the prisoners twice on the way out: once before they unbolted the gates, to make sure they were safe in opening them, and again when the gates had been opened and the prisoners were passing through. And if they thought they'd miscounted, they recounted outside the gates.)

"To hell with the mortar," said Tiurin, with a gesture of impatience. "Sling it over the wall."

"Don't wait, leader. Go ahead, you're needed there. (Shukhov usually addressed Tiurin, more respectfully, as Andrei Pro-kofievich but now, after working like that, he felt equal to the team-leader. He didn't put it to himself 'Look, I'm your equal', he just knew it.) And as Tiurin strode down the ramp he called after him, jokingly: "Why do these rats make the work-day so short? We're just getting into our stride when they call it off."

Shukhov was left alone now with Senka. You couldn't say much to him. Besides, you didn't have to tell him things: he was the wisest of them all, he understood without need of words.

Slap on the mortar. Down with the blocks. Press it home. See it's straight. Mortar. Block. Mortar. Block. . . .

Wasn't it enough that Tiurin had told them himself not to bother about the mortar? Just throw it over the wall and —— off. But Shukhov wasn't made that way: eight years in a camp couldn't change his nature. He worried about anything he could make use of, about every scrap of work he could do—nothing must be wasted without good reason.

Mortar. Block. Mortar. Block. . . .

"Finish, —— you," shouted Senka. "Let's hop it."

He picked up a barrow and ran down the ramp.

But Shukhov—and if the guards had put the dogs on him it would have made no difference—ran to the back and looked about. Not bad. Then he ran and gave the wall a good look over, to the left, to the right. His eye was as accurate as a spirit level. Straight and even. His hands were as young as ever. He dashed down the ramp.

Senka was already out of the mortar-shop and running down the slope.

"Come on, come on," he shouted over his shoulder.

"Run on. I'll catch up," Shukhov gestured.

But he went into the mortar-shop. He couldn't simply throw his trowel down. He might not be there the next day. They might send the team off to the Socialist Way of Life settlement. It could be six months before he returned to the power-station. But did that mean he was to throw down his trowel? If he'd pinched it he had to hang on to it.

Both the stoves had been doused. It was dark, frightening. Frightening not because it was dark but because everyone had left, because he alone might be missing at the count by the gates, and the guards would beat him.

Yet his eyes darted here, darted there, and, spotting a big stone in the corner, he pulled it aside, slipped his trowel under it, and hid it. So that's that.

Now to catch up with Senka. Senka had stopped after running a hundred paces or so. Senka would never leave anyone in a jam. Answer for it? Then together.

They ran level, the tall and the short. Senka was a head taller than Shukhov, and a big head it was too.

There are loafers who race one another of their own free will round a stadium. Those devils should be running after a full day's work, with aching back and wet mittens and worn-out valenki—and in the cold too.

They panted like mad dogs. All you could hear was their hoarse breathing.

Well, Tiurin was at the gates. He'd explain.

They were running straight into the crowd. Frightening it was.

Hundreds of throats booing you at once, and cursing you up hill and down dale. Wouldn't *you* be scared if you had five hundred men blowing off their tops at you?

But what about the guards? That was the chief thing.

No. No trouble with them. Tiurin was there, in the last row. He must have explained. Taken the blame on his own shoulders.

But the lads yelled, the lads swore. And what swearing! Even

Senka couldn't help hearing and, drawing a deep breath, gave back as good as he got. He'd kept quiet all his life—but now, how he bellowed! Raised his fists too, ready to pick a scrap right away. The men fell silent. Someone laughed.

"Hey, one hundred and fourth," came a shout. "Your deaf'un's a fake. We've just tested him."

Everyone laughed. The guards too.

"Form fives."

They didn't open the gates. They didn't trust themselves. They pushed the crowd back from the gates (everyone stuck to the gates like idiots—as if they'd get out quicker that way!)

"Form fives. First. Second. Third. . . ."

Each five, as it was called, took a few paces forward.

While Shukhov was recovering his breath he looked up. The moon had risen and was frowning, crimson-faced. Yesterday at this hour it had stood much higher.

Pleased that everything had gone so smoothly, Shukhov nudged the captain in the ribs and said:

"Listen, captain, where according to this science of yours does the old moon go afterwards?"

"Where does it go? What d'you mean? What ignorance! It's simply not visible."

Shukhov shook his head and laughed.

"Well, if it's not visible, how d'you know it's there?"

"So, according to you," said the captain, unable to believe his ears, "every month it's another moon."

"What's strange about that? People are born every day. Why not a moon every four weeks?"

"Phugh!" said the captain and spat. "I've never met a sailor as stupid as you in my life. So where do *you* think the old moon goes?"

"That's what I'm asking you. Where does it go?" Shukhov showed his teeth in a smile.

"Well, tell me. Where does it go?"

Shukhov sighed and said with a slight lisp:

"In our village, folk say God crumbles up the old moon into stars."

"What savages!" The captain laughed. "I've never heard that. Then you believe in God, Shukhov?"

"Why not?" asked Shukhov, surprised. "Hear Him thunder and try not to believe in Him."

"But why does God do it?"

"Do what?"

"Crumble the moon into stars. Why?"

"Well, can't you understand?" said Shukhov. "The stars fall down and then. The gaps have to be filled."

"Turn round, you scum," a guard shouted. "Get in line."

The count had almost reached them. The twelfth five of the fifth hundred had moved ahead, leaving only Buinovsky and Shukhov at the back.

The escort was worried. There was a discussion over the counting boards. Somebody missing. Again somebody missing. Why the hell can't they learn to count?

They'd counted 462. Ought to be 463.

Once more they pushed everybody back from the gates (the zeks had crowded forward again.)

"Form fives. First. Second. . . ."

What made this recounting so devilish was that the time wasted on it was the zeks' own, not the authorities'. They would still have to cross the steppe, get to the camp and queue up there to be searched. The columns would come in from all sides at the double, trying to be first at the frisking and into the camp. The column that was back first was cock o' the roost in the camp that evening: the mess-hall was theirs, they were first in the parcels queue, first at the private kitchen, first at the C.E.D. to pick up letters or hand in their own to be censored, first at the sick-bay, the barber's, the baths—first everywhere.

And the escort too's in a hurry to get the zeks in and be off for the night. A soldier's life isn't much fun either: a lot of work, little time.

And now the count had come out wrong.

As the last few fives were called forward Shukhov began to hope that there were going to be three in the last row after all. No, damn it, two again.

The tellers went to the head-guard with their tally-boards. There was a consultation. The head-guard shouted:

"Team-leader of the 104th."

Tiurin took a half pace forward.

81

"Here."

"Did you leave anyone behind in the power-station? Think."

"No."

"Think again. I'll knock your head off. . . ."

"No, I'm quite sure."

But he stole a glance at Pavlo. Could anyone have dropped off to sleep in the mortar-shop?

"Form up in teams," the head-guard shouted.

They had formed the groups of five just as they happened to be standing. Now they began to shift about. Voices boomed out: "Seventy-fifth over here," "This way, thirteenth," "Thirty-second here."

The 104th, being all in the rear, formed up there too. They were empty-handed to a man, Shukhov noticed; in their daftness they'd worked on so late they'd collected no firewood. Only two of them were carrying small bundles.

This game was played every evening: before work was over the proles would gather chips, sticks, and broken laths, and tie them together with bits of string or ragged tapes to carry back with them. The first raid on their bundles would take place near the gates to the work-site. If either the superintendent or one of the foremen was standing there, he'd order the prisoners to throw down their firewood (millions of roubles had gone up in smoke, yet there they were thinking they'd make up the losses with kindling-chips). But a zek calculated his own way: if everyone brought even a few sticks back with him the barracks would be warmer. Barrack-orderlies were issued five kilograms of coal-dust a stove and little heat could be squeezed out of that. So the men would break up the sticks or saw them short and slip them under their coats.

The escort never made the zeks drop their firewood at the gates to the work-site. For one thing, it would have been an offence to the uniform; and secondly they had their hands on the tommy-guns, ready to shoot with them. But just before entering the zone several ranks in the column were ordered to throw their stuff down. The escort, however, robbed mercifully: they had to leave something for the guards, and for the zeks themselves, who otherwise wouldn't bring any with them.

So every zek brought some firewood along with him every

evening. You never knew when you might get it through or when they'd snaffle it.

While Shukhov was scouring the ground in search of a few chips, Tiurin had finished counting the team.

"One hundred and fourth all present", he reported to the head-guard.

Just then Tsezar rejoined his own team from the group of office-workers. His pipe was glowing as he puffed away at it; his dark moustache was tipped with frost.

"Well, captain, how are things?" he asked.

A man who's warm can't understand a man who's freezing. "How are things?" What a damn fool question!

"You may well ask," said the captain, his shoulders sagging. "Worked so hard I can hardly straighten my back."

You might give me something to smoke was what he meant.

Tsezar gave him something to smoke. The captain was the only man in the team he stuck to. He could unburden his heart to him: to no one else.

"There's a man missing from the thirty-second. From the thirty-second," everybody began to mutter.

The deputy team-leader of the 32nd scurried off with another young fellow to search the repair-shops. And in the crowd people kept asking: Who? How? Where? Soon it reached Shukhov's ears that it was the dark little Moldavian who was missing. The Moldavian? Not the one who, it was said, had been a Rumanian spy, a real spy?

You could find up to five spies in each team. But they were fakes, prison-made spies. They passed as spies in their dossiers, but really they were simply ex-p.o.w.s. Shukhov himself was one of these "spies".

But the Moldavian was genuine.

The head of the escort ran his eye down the list and grew black in the face. After all, if the spy were to escape what would happen to the head of the escort?

In the crowd everybody, including Shukhov, flew into a rage. Were they going through all this for that shit, that slimy little snake, that stinking bug? The sky was already quite dark; what light there was came from the moon. You could see the stars—this meant the frost was gathering its strength for the night

—and that undersized bastard was missing. What, haven't you had your bellyful of work, you miserable wretch? Isn't the official spell of eleven hours, dawn to dusk, long enough for you? Just you wait, the prosecutor will add something.

Odd that anyone could work so hard as to ignore the signal to knock off.

He completely forgot that he'd been working like that himself only an hour ago—that he'd been annoyed with the others for assembling at the gate too early. Now he was chilled to the bone and his fury mounted with everyone else's; were they to be kept waiting another half-hour by that Moldavian? If the guards handed him over to the zeks they'd tear him apart, like wolves with a lamb.

Aye, the cold was coming into its own now. No one stood quiet. They either stamped their feet where they stood or walked two or three paces to and fro.

People were discussing whether the Moldavian could have escaped. Well, if he'd bolted during the day that was one thing, but if he'd hidden and was simply waiting for the sentries to go off the watch-towers he hadn't a chance. Unless he'd left a trail through the wire the sentries wouldn't be allowed back in camp for at least three days. They'd have to go on manning the towers for a week, if necessary. That was in the regulations, as the old-timers knew. In short, if someone escaped it was all up with the guards; they were hounded, without sleep or food. Sometimes they were roused to such fury that the runaway wouldn't get back alive.

Tsezar was arguing with the captain:

"For instance, when he hung his pince-nez on the ship's rigging. D'you remember?"

"Hm, yes," the captain said as he smoked.

"Or the perambulator on the steps. Bumping down and down."

"Yes. . . . But the scenes on board are somewhat artificial."

"Well, you see, we've been spoiled by modern camera-technique."

"And the maggots in the meat, they crawl about like rainworms. Surely they weren't that size?"

"What do you expect of the cinema? You can't show them smaller."

84

"Well, if they were to bring that meat here to our camp instead of the fish they're feeding us on and dumped it straight into the cauldron we'd be only too . . ."

The prisoners howled.

Three small figures were bursting out of the repair-shop. So they'd found the Moldavian.

"Boooo!" went the crowd at the gates.

And they yelled, as the group drew nearer:

"Rat! Shit! Twirp! Cow's twat! Son of a poxy bitch!"

And Shukhov joined in:

"You rat!"

It's no trifle to rob five hundred men of over half an hour.

Ducking his head, the Moldavian ran like a mouse.

"Halt!" a guard shouted. And, noting down "K 460", said: "Where were you?"

He strode over to the man and turned the butt of his carbine at him.

In the crowd people were still hurling curses: "Skunk! Pest! Swine!"

But others, seeing the guard make ready to swing his carbine, held their tongues.

The Moldavian could hardly keep on his feet. He backed from the guard.

The deputy team-leader of the 32nd advanced.

"He crawled up to do some plastering, the wretch. Trying to hide from me! Warmed up there and fell asleep."

And he hit the man hard in the face and on the neck, pushing him further from the guard.

The Moldavian reeled back, and as he did so a Hungarian, one of his team-mates, leaped up at him and kicked him hard from behind.

That wasn't like spying. Any fool can spy. A spy has a clean, exciting life. But try and spend ten years in a hard-labour camp!

The guard lowered his carbine.

The head of the escort shouted:

"Back from the gates. Form fives."

Another recount, the dogs. Why should they count us now that everything's clear? The prisoners began to boo. All their anger switched from the Moldavian to the escort. They booed and didn't move.

85

"W-wha-a-at?" shouted the head of the escort. "Want to sit down on the snow? All right, I'll have you down in a minute. I'll keep you here till dawn."

He was quite capable of doing it too. He'd had them on the snow many a time. "Down on your faces!" And, to the escort: "Release safety-catches!" The zeks knew all about that. They drew back from the gates.

"Back, back!" yelled the escort.

"What's the sense of pushing up to the gates anyhow, you crapping idiots?" men barked from the rear at the men in front as they were pushed back.

"Form fives. First. Second. Third. . . ."

Now the moon was shining at the full. It cast its light all around and the crimson tint had gone. It had climbed a quarter of the way up the sky. The evening was lost. That damned Moldavian. Those damned guards. This damned life.

As the prisoners in front were counted they turned and stood on tiptoe to see whether there were two men or three in the back row. It was a matter of life or death to them now.

Shukhov had the feeling that there were going to be four. He was stupefied with fear. One extra. Another recount. But it turned out that Fetiukov, after cadging a fag-end from the captain, had been dithering and had failed to get into his five in time. So now he'd turned up in the back row as if he were an extra.

A guard struck Fetiukov angrily on the back of the neck.

Serve him right.

So they counted three in the back row. The count had come out right, thank God.

"Back from the gates" shouted a guard at the top of his voice. But this time the zeks didn't mutter: they'd noticed soldiers coming out of the guard-house and cordoning off an area the other side of the gates.

So they were going to be let out.

None of the foremen were in sight, not the superintendent, so the prisoners kept their firewood.

The gates swung open. And now the head of the escort, accompanied by a checker, came and stood on the other side, near some wooden railings.

"First. Second. Third. . . ."

If the numbers tallied again the sentries would be removed from the watch-towers.

But what a distance they had to tramp along the edge of the site to reach the towers at the far end of it! It was only when the last prisoner had been led off the site and the numbers had been found to tally that they'd telephone all the towers and relieve the sentries. If the head of the escort had his wits about him he'd put the column on the move right away, for he knew the zeks had nowhere to run to and that the sentries would overtake the column. But some of the guards were so foolish, they feared they hadn't enough troops for handling the zeks: so they waited.

They had one of those blockheads this evening.

A whole day in that freezing cold! The zeks were already chilled to the marrow: and now to stand about another shivering hour, when work was over! Yet it wasn't so much the cold and the fact that they'd lost an evening that infuriated them: the point was, there'd be no time now to do anything of their own in the camp.

"How is it you happen to know life in the British Navy so well?" Shukhov heard someone in the next five asking.

"Well you see, I spent nearly a month on board a British cruiser. Had my own cabin. I was attached to a convoy as liaison officer. And imagine: after the war the British admiral—only the devil could have put the idea into his head—sent me a gift, a souvenir as 'a token of gratitude', curse him! I was absolutely aghast. And now here we are, all lumped together. It's pretty steep being imprisoned here with Bendera's men. . . ."

Strange! Yes, a strange sight indeed: the naked steppe, the empty building-site, the snow gleaming in the moon-light. And the escort guards: they'd gone to their posts, ten paces apart, guns at the ready. And the black herd of prisoners: and among them, in a black coat like all the rest, a man, S 311, who'd never imagined life without gold shoulder-straps, had hobnobbed with a British admiral and now sweated at a barrow with Fetiukov.

You can push a man this way, and you can push a man that way.

Now the escort was ready. This time without any "prayer" the head-guard barked at them:

"Quick march! Make it snappy!"

To hell with your "Make it snappy"! All the other columns were ahead of them. What sense was there in hurrying? The prisoners didn't have to be in league with one another to tumble to the situation: You kept us back, now it's our turn. The escort too, after all, was dying for a warm corner.

"Step out!" shouted the guard. "Step out, you in front."

To hell with your "Step out". The zeks marched with measured tread, hanging their heads as at a funeral. Now we've nothing to lose: we'd be the last back anyhow. He wouldn't treat us like human beings, now let him burst himself shouting.

On he went, "Step out! Step out!". But he realized it was futile. He couldn't order his men to shoot either. The prisoners were marching in fives, keeping in line, all correct. He had no power to hound them faster. (When they marched out to work in the morning the zeks walked slowly, to spare themselves. A man who's in a hurry won't live to see the end of his stretch—he'll tire and be done for.)

So on with regular, deliberate steps. The snow crunched under their boots. Some of them talked in low voices, others walked in silence. Shukhov asked himself whether there was anything he'd left undone in the camp that morning. Ah, the sick-bay. Funny, he'd forgotten all about the sick-bay while he'd been working.

This must be round about the consulting hour. He'd manage it if he skipped his supper. But now somehow his back wasn't aching and his temperature wouldn't be high enough. A waste of time. He'd pull through without benefit of the doctor. The only cure those docs know is to put you in your grave.

It wasn't the sick-bay that appealed to him now, it was the prospect of adding something to his supper. His hopes were all pinned on that long-overdue parcel of Tsezar's.

A sudden change came over the column. It began to sway, to break out of its regular stride. The prisoners heaved forward with a buzz of excitement. And now the tail five, which included Shukhov, was no longer treading on the heels of the five in front, it had to run to keep up. A few more paces, and again it was running.

When the rear of the column spilled over a rise Shukhov saw to the right, far away across the steppe, another dark column on the move, marching diagonally across their course. They, too, seemed to be forcing their pace.

It must be from the machine-works, that column: there were about three hundred men in it. Another lot out of luck! Must have been held up—Shukhov wondered why. To finish assembling some piece of machinery? They could be kept after work-hours for that. But what did it matter to them? They worked all day in the warmth.

Who'd get in first? The lads ran, just ran. Even the escort broke into a jog-trot: only the head-guard remembered to shout "Don't straggle. Keep up there, you in the rear. Keep up."

Oh, shut your trap. . . . What are you yapping about? As if we wouldn't keep up!

They forgot to talk; they forgot to think; everyone in the column was obsessed by one idea: to get back first.

Things were so lumped together, the sweet and the sour, that the prisoners saw the escort itself, now, as friend rather than foe. Now the enemy was the other column.

Their spirits rose, their anger passed.

"Get a move on, get a move on!" the rear shouted to the front.

Now our column had reached the street, while the other had passed out of sight behind the blocks of houses. They'd been racing blindly.

It was easier for us now, we were running down the middle of the street. And our escort had less to stumble over at the sides. This was where we ought to gain ground.

There was another reason why we simply had to reach the camp gates first: the guards there were unusually slow in searching the column from the machine-works. Ever since zeks had begun cutting one another's throats in the camp the authorities had been coming to one conclusion: that knives were being made at the machine-works and smuggled in. So the zeks who worked there were gone over with special thoroughness on return to the camp. In late autumn, when the earth was already cold, the guards would shout at them:

"Off with your boots, machine-works team! Hold your boots in your hands."

And would frisk them barefoot.

Or, despite the frost, they'd pick men out at random, shouting: "You there, take off your right boot. And you, take off your left!"

A zek would pull off his boot and, hopping on one foot, turn it upside down and shake out the foot-cloth. No knife, damn you!

Shukhov had heard—he didn't know whether it was true or not

—that back in the summer the zeks from the machine-works had brought back two poles for a volley-ball net and that all the knives were there inside them. Ten long knives in each pole. And now knives would turn up occasionally, here and there.

So it was at a jog-trot that they passed the new club and the residential block and the wood-processing plant, and reached the turning that led straight on to the gates.

"Hoooooo-ooo" shouted the whole column, in unison.

That was the turning we'd aimed at reaching before the others. The rival column was a hundred and fifty paces behind, on our right.

Now we could take things easy. Everyone was delighted. As delighted as a hare when it finds it can still terrify a frog.

There lay the camp, just as we'd left it in the morning: lights were on in the zone over the thick fence, specially powerful ones in front of the guard-house. The entire area was flooded with light; it was as bright as day. They had to have it like that when they frisked us.

But we hadn't reached the gates yet.

"Halt!" shouted a guard and, handing his tommy-gun to a soldier, ran up close to the column (they weren't allowed to do that with their guns). "All those on the right carrying firewood dump it to their right."

He didn't have to guess about the firewood, the zeks were carrying it quite openly. A bundle fell, a second, a third. Some would have liked to conceal a stick or two inside the column, but their neighbours objected:

"Throw it down as you're told! D'you want others to lose theirs because of you?"

Who's the zek's main enemy? Another zek. If only they weren't at loggerheads with one another—ah, what a difference that'd make!

"Quick march," shouted the head-guard.

They advanced towards the gates.

Here five roads converged. An hour earlier all the other columns had met here. If they were paved, these roads, this would be just the place for the main square of a future city: and then processions would meet here, just as now columns of zeks did as they poured in from every direction, with sentries and guards all about.

The guards were already warming themselves indoors. They came out and formed a cordon across the road.

"Unbutton your coats. Unbutton your jackets."

They pulled the zeks' arms apart, the better to hug them and slap their sides. Same as in the morning, more or less.

It isn't so terrible to unbutton your coat now. We're going home.

That's what everyone used to say: "Going home."

We never had time to think of any other home.

While the head of the column was being frisked, Shukhov went over to Tsezar:

"Tsezar Markovich, I'll run straight to the parcels office and keep a place in the queue for you."

Tsezar turned. The fringe of his dark moustache was tipped with frost.

"Why should you do that, Ivan Denisovich? Perhaps there won't be a parcel."

"Oh well, if there isn't what harm's done? I'll wait ten minutes, anyway. If you don't turn up I'll go to the hut."

(Shukhov reckoned like this: if Tsezar didn't come, maybe someone else would; then he could sell him his place in the queue.)

Obviously Tzesar was longing for his parcel.

"Very well, Ivan Denisovich, run ahead and keep a place for me. Wait ten minutes, no longer."

And now Shukhov was on the point of being frisked. Today he had nothing to conceal. He would step forward fearlessly. He slowly unbuttoned his coat and undid the canvas belt round his wadded jacket, and although he couldn't remember having anything forbidden, eight years in camp had given him the habit of caution: he thrust a hand into his knee-pocket to make sure it was empty.

And there lay a small piece of broken hacksaw-blade, the tiny length of steel that he'd picked up in his thriftiness at the building-site without any intention of bringing it to camp.

He hadn't meant to bring it, but now, what a pity to throw it away! Why, he could make a little knife out of it, very handy for cobbling or tailoring!

If he'd intended to bring it with him he'd have thought hard of where to conceal it. But now the guards were only two rows ahead and the first of these rows was already stepping forward to be searched.

His choice had to be swift as the wind. Should he take cover

91

behind the row in front of him and toss the bit of metal in the snow (it'd be noticed but they wouldn't know who the culprit was) or keep it on him?

For that strip of hacksaw he could get ten days in the cells, if they classed it as a knife.

But a cobbling knife was money, it was bread.

A pity to throw it away.

He slipped it into his left mitten.

At that moment the next row was ordered to step forward and be searched.

Now the last three men stood in full view—Senka, Shukhov and the lad from the 32nd team who had gone to look for the Moldavian.

Because they were three and the guards facing them were five, Shukhov could try a ruse. He could choose which of the two guards on the right to present himself to. He decided against a young ruddy-faced one and plumped for an older man with a grey moustache. The older one, of course, was experienced and would find the blade easily if he wanted to, but because of his age he must have got fed up with the work. It must stink in his nostrils by now like burning sulphur.

Meanwhile Shukhov had removed both mittens, the empty one and the one with the hacksaw, and held them in one hand (the empty one in front) together with the untied rope-belt. He fully unbuttoned his jacket, lifted high the edges of his coat and jacket (never had he been so servile at the search but now he wanted to show he was innocent —Come on, frisk me!), and at the word of command stepped forward.

The guard slapped Shukhov's sides and back, and the outside of his knee-pocket. Nothing there. He kneaded the edges of coat and jacket. Nothing there either. He was about to pass him through when, for safety's sake, he crushed the mitten that Shukhov held out to him—the empty one.

The guard crushed it in his hand, and Shukhov felt as though pincers of iron were crushing everything inside him. One such squeeze on the other mitten and he'd be sunk—the cells on three hundred grams of bread a day and hot skilly one day in three. He imagined how weak he'd grow, how difficult he'd find it to get back to his present condition, neither fed nor starving.

And an urgent prayer rose in his heart:

"Oh Lord, save me! Don't let them send me to the cells."

And while all this raced through his mind, the guard, after finishing with the right-hand mitten, stretched a hand out to deal with the other (he would have squeezed them at the same moment if Shukhov had held them in separate hands). Just then the guard heard his chief, who was in a hurry to get on, shout to the escort:

"Come along, bring up the machine-works column."

And instead of examining the other mitten the old guard waved Shukhov on. He was through.

He ran off to catch up with the others. They had already formed fives in a sort of corridor between long beams, like horse-lines in a market, a sort of paddock for prisoners. He ran lightly, hardly feeling the ground. He didn't say a prayer of thanksgiving because he hadn't time, and anyway it would have been out of place.

The escort now drew aside. They were only waiting for their chief. They had gathered for their own use all the firewood the 104th had dumped before being frisked: what the guards had removed during the frisking itself was heaped near the guard-house.

The moon had risen still higher; the cold grew keener in the pale bright night.

The head-guard walked to the sentry-house: he had to get a receipt for the four hundred and sixty-three prisoners. He spoke briefly to Priakhov, Volkovoi's deputy.

"K 460", shouted Priakhov.

The Moldavian, who had buried himself deep in the column, drew in his breath and went over to the right of the corridor. He was still hanging his head and his shoulders were hunched.

"Come here," Priakhov ordered, gesturing him to walk round the column.

The Moldavian did so. He was ordered to stand there, his arms behind his back.

That meant they were going to charge him with attempting to escape. They'd put him in the cells.

Just in front of the gates, right and left of the "paddock", stood two guards. The gates, thrice the height of a man, opened slowly. The command rang out:

"Form fives!" (No need here to order the zeks back from the

gates; all the gates opened inwards, into the zone. Let the zeks mass as they wished and push against the gates from within, they wouldn't be able to break out.) "First. Second. Third. . . ."

It was at the evening recount on their return through the gates that the prisoners, freezing and famished, found the icy wind hardest to bear. A bowl of thin cabbage soup, all scorched up, was as grateful to them as rain to parched earth. They'd swallow it in one gulp. That bowl of soup—it was dearer than freedom, dearer than life itself, past, present and future.

They passed through the gates, those zeks, like soldiers back from a campaign, brisk, taut, eager—clear the road for 'em.

For a trusty with a cushy job at staff quarters, those prisoners on the march must have been something to think about!

After the recount a prisoner became a free man again—for the first time in the day since the guards had given them the morning signal to muster. They passed through the big gates (of the zone), through the small gates (of the intermediate zone), through two more gates (on the mustering-ground)—and then they could scatter where they liked.

But not the team-leaders. They were caught by the officer who assigned them their work: "All team-leaders to the planning office."

Shukhov rushed past the prison, between the huts, to the parcels-office. Tsezar, meanwhile, went at a dignified, even pace in the opposite direction, to where people were swarming round a pole with a board nailed to it. On it was the name of anyone for whom a parcel was waiting, written in indelible pencil.

Most writing in the camp was done on plywood, not on paper. It was surer, somehow, more reliable. The guards and turnkeys used wood, too, for keeping tally of the zeks. You can scrape it clean for the next day, and use it again. Economical.

Zeks who stay in camp all day can put themselves, among other odd jobs, to reading the names on the board, meeting people who've got a parcel as they come in from work, and giving them the number. Not much of a job, but it can earn you a cigarette.

Shukhov ran to the parcels-office—a little annexe to a hut, to which in turn a small porch had been added. The porch had no door and was open to the weather. All the same, it was cosier that way; it had a roof, after all.

A queue had formed along the walls of the porch. Shukhov

joined it. There were some fifteen ahead of him. That meant over an hour's wait, to just before locking-up time. And there were others who'd be behind him in the queue—the zeks of the power-house column who'd gone to look for their names on the board, and the machine-works column too. Looked as though *they* would have to come again. Tomorrow morning.

People stood in the queue with little bags and sacks. On the other side of the door (Shukhov himself hadn't ever received a parcel at this camp but he knew from hearsay) guards opened the parcels, which came packed in wooden boxes, with hatchets. They took everything out and examined the contents. They cut, they broke, they fingered. They tipped things out from one container into another. If there was anything liquid, in glass jars or tins, they opened them and poured it out, though you had nothing but your hands or a cloth-bag to hold it in. They didn't give you the jars, they were scared of something. If there was anything home-baked, or some tasty sweet-meats or sausage or smoked fish, the guard would take a bite at it himself. (And just you try to get uppish and grouse, and they'll immediately say that this and that are forbidden and won't issue them to you at all.) Every zek who got a parcel had to give and give, starting with the guard who opened it. And when they'd finished their search they didn't give you the stuff in the box it had come in, they just swept everything into your bag, even into the skirt of your coat and . . . off you go. Sometimes they'd whisk you out so fast you'd be sure to leave something behind. No good going back for it. It wouldn't be there.

When he was in Ust-Izhma Shukhov had got parcels a couple of times. But he wrote to his wife that it was a waste—don't send them. Don't take the food out of the kids' mouths.

Although when he had been at liberty Shukhov had found it easier to feed his whole family than it ever was to feed himself now, he knew what those parcels cost. He knew too that his family wouldn't be able to keep it up for ten years. Better do without them.

But though he'd decided that way, every time someone in the team, or close by in the barracks, received a parcel (which was almost every day) his heart ached because there wasn't one for him. And though he'd strictly forbidden his wife to send him anything even for Easter, and though he never thought of reading the list except for a rich team-mate, every now and then he felt himself longing for someone to run up and say:

"Shukhov! Why don't you go for your parcel? There's one for you."

But no one ran up.

He had less and less cause to remember Temgenovo and his home there. Life in camp wore him out from reveille to bed-time, with not a second for idle reflections.

Now as he stood among the men who were buoying themselves up with the hope of soon digging their teeth into bits of pork-fat, of spreading butter on their bread or sweetening their mugs of tea with lumps of sugar, Shukhov had one wish only—to reach the mess-hall in time and to eat his skilly hot. It was only half as good when it was cold.

He reckoned that if his name hadn't turned up on the list Tsezar would long ago have gone back to the barracks to wash. But if he'd found it there he would now be collecting bags, plastic mugs and a basin. That would take him ten minutes. And Shukhov had promised to wait.

There in the queue Shukhov learned some news. Again there wasn't going to be a Sunday this week; again they were going to pinch one of their Sundays. He, like everyone else, had expected it, for if there happened to be five Sundays in a month, they gave them three and made them work the other two. Shukhov had expected it, but when he heard it a spasm of pain caught his heart: who wouldn't begrudge the loss of that sweet day? Though what they were saying in the queue was right: they knew how to chivvy them even on Sundays. They'd invent something—fixing up the baths, or building a wall somewhere, or cleaning up the yard. There were mattresses to be changed and shaken, bed-bugs in the bunk-frames to be exterminated. Or they'd have the idea of checking you with your photo. Or of carrying out an inventory: turning you with all your things into the yard and keeping you there half the day.

Nothing seems to make the authorities madder than zeks kipping quietly after breakfast.

The queue was moving, though slowly. People were coming in and jumping it without a by-your-leave, just elbowing through to the front—a camp-barber, a book-keeper, a man who worked in the C.E.D. But they weren't rank-and-file, they were respectable trusties, swine of the first order with cushy jobs in the camp. The zeks who worked outside thought them lower than shit (a rating the trusties returned). But it was futile to protest: the trusties were a gang on their own, and were also well in with the guards.

Now there were only ten ahead of Shukhov. Another seven had hurried in to line up behind him, when Tsezar, stooping, appeared in the doorway, wearing the new fur hat that had been sent him from outside.

Now take that hat. Tsezar must have tickled someone's palm to get permission for wearing a town-hat so clean and new. They even robbed others of their bedraggled service-hats. Here, wear the camp pig-fur model!

A queer fellow with glasses was standing in the queue, his head buried in a newspaper. Tsezar at once made for him:

"Aha, Pyotr Mikhailych."

They blossomed like a couple of poppies. The queer fellow said: "Look what I've got! A fresh *Vechorka*.[1] They sent it by airmail."

"Really," said Tsezar, sticking his nose into the newspaper. How on earth could they make out such tiny print in the glimmer of that miserable lamp?

"There's a most fascinating review of a Zavadsky première."

Those Muscovites can smell one another at a distance, like dogs: they sniff and sniff when they meet, in a way of their own. They jabber so fast too, each trying to out-talk the other. When they're jabbering away like that you hear practically no Russian: they might be talking Latvian or Rumanian.

However, Tsezar had got all his bags with him: everything in order.

"So I can ... er ... Tsezar Markovich," lisped Shukhov, "I'll be off now."

"Of course, of course," said Tsezar, raising his dark moustache above the top of the newspaper. "Tell me though, who am I after? And who's after me?"

Shukhov told him his place in the queue and then, with a gentle hint, asked:

"Shall I bring you your supper?"

[1] Veehernaya Moskva—an evening newspaper.

97

(That meant from the mess-hall to the hut, in a mess-tin. This was strictly against the rules—there'd been many about it. When they caught you they poured your food out of the mess-tin on to the ground and put you in the lock-up. All the same, food was carried and would go on being carried, because if a zek has anything to do he'll never find time to go to the mess-hall with his team.)

Shukhov asked: 'Shall I bring you your supper?', but murmured to himself: "Surely he's not going to be stingy? Won't he give me his supper? After all, there's no kasha for supper, only thin skilly."

"No, no," said Tsezar with a smile. "Eat it yourself, Ivan Denisovich."

That was just what Shukhov was expecting. And now, like a bird on the wing, he darted from the porch and—across the zone, across the zone.

The prisoners were scurrying in all directions. There was a time when the camp commandant had issued yet another order: on no account were prisoners to walk about the camp on their own. Wherever possible, a team was to go intact. But when there could be no business for a whole team to do at once—at the sickbay, say, or at the latrines—then groups of four or five were to be formed and a senior appointed to head them and take them there and back in a body.

The camp commandant took a very firm stand on that order. No one dared contradict him. The guards picked up solitary prisoners, took down their numbers, yanked them off to the cells—yet the order was a flop. It flopped quietly, like many much-heralded orders. Someone, say, is sent for by the security boys—must you take another four or five with you? Or you have to get your food from the store. Why the hell should I go with you? Someone has the strange idea of going to the C.E.D. to read newspapers. Who wants to go with him? And this fellow goes to have his boots mended, another to the drying-shed, a third merely from one hut to another (that's forbidden more strictly than anything else)—how can you hold them all back?

With that rule of his the commandant would have robbed them of their last shred of freedom, but it didn't work out, much as he tried, the big-bellied swine.

Hurrying along the path, meeting a guard on the way and,

to be on the safe side, taking off his hat to him, Shukhov ran into the hut. The place was in an uproar: someone's bread ration had been snitched during the day and the poor fellow was shouting at the orderlies and the orderlies were shouting back. But the 104th's corner was empty.

Shukhov was always thankful if on returning to camp he found that his mattress hadn't been turned over and that the guards hadn't been snooping around. So that's all right.

He dashed to his bunk, taking off his coat as he ran. Up with the coat, up with the mittens and the nice bit of blade. He probed the depths of his mattress—the bread was there. Good for him he'd sewn it in.

And out he ran. To the mess-hall.

He reached it without meeting a guard—only a couple of zeks arguing over their bread ration.

Outside the moon shone brighter than ever. The lamps seemed to be paler now. The barracks cast deep shadows. The door to the mess-hall lay beyond a broad porch with four steps. Now the porch too lay in shadow. But above it a small lamp was swaying, and creaking dismally in the cold. The light it cast was rainbow-hued, from the frost maybe, or the dirt on the glass.

The camp commandant had issued yet another strict order: the teams were to enter the mess-hall in double file. To this he added: on reaching the steps they were to stay there and not climb on to the porch; they were to form up in fives and remain standing until the mess-orderly gave them the go-ahead.

The post of mess-orderly was firmly held by "the Limper". Because of his lameness he'd managed to get classed as disabled, but he was a hefty son of a bitch. He'd got himself a cudgel of birch, and standing on the porch would clout anyone who came up without his say-so. No, not anyone. He was smart, and could tell, even in the dark, when it was better to let a man be—anyone who might give him tit for tat. He hit the down-and-outs. Once he hit Shukhov.

He was called an orderly. But, looking closer into it, he was a real prince: he hobnobbed with the cooks.

Today all the teams may have turned up together or there may have been delay in getting things shipshape, but there was quite a crowd on the porch. Among them was the Limper, with his assistant. The mess-chief himself was there too. They were handling the crowd without guards—the toughs.

The mess-chief was a fat swine with a head like a pumpkin and a mighty pair of shoulders. He was bursting with energy and when he walked he seemed nothing but a lot of jerks, with springs for arms and legs. He wore a white lambskin hat without a number on it, finer than any civilian's. And his waistcoat was lambskin to match, with a number on it, true, but hardly bigger than a postage stamp—a tribute to Volkovoi. He bore no number at all on his back. He respected no one and all the zeks were afraid of him. He held the lives of thousands in his hands. Once they'd tried to beat him up but all the cooks—choice thugs they were—had leaped to his defence.

Shukhov would be in the soup if the 104th had already gone in. The Limper knew everyone by sight and, with his chief present, wouldn't think of letting a man in with the wrong team, he'd make a point of chivvying him.

Prisoners had been known to slip in behind the Limper's back by climbing over the porch-railings. Shukhov had done it too. But tonight, under the chief's very nose, that was out of the question—he'd clout you such a one that you'd only just manage to drag yourself off to the doctor.

Nip along to the porch and see whether, among all those identical black coats, the 104th was still there.

He got there just as the men began shoving (what could they do? it would soon be time to turn in) as though they were storming a stronghold—the first step, the second, the third, the fourth. Got there! They poured on to the porch.

"Stop, you ——," the Limper shouted and raised his cudgel at the men in front. "Get back or I'll smash your mugs."

"What can we do about it?" they yelled back at him. "The fellows at the back are pushing us."

That was true, but the lot up in front were offering little resistance. They hoped to dash through into the mess-hall.

The Limper put his cudgel across his chest—it might have been a barricade in a street-battle—and rushed, might and main, at the men in front. His assistant, the trusty, shared the cudgel with him, and so did the mess-chief—who might deign, he'd apparently decided, to soil his hands with it.

They pushed hard: they had plenty of vim, with all that meat in them. The zeks reeled back. The men in front toppled down on to the men behind them, bowled them over like standing sheaves.

"You —— Limper, we'll settle with you," cried a man in the crowd, hiding behind the others. As for the rest, they fell without a word, they got up without a word: as quick as they could, before being trodden on.

The steps were clear. The mess-chief went back to the porch but the Limper stayed at the top.

"Form fives, muttonheads," he shouted. "How many times have I told you I'll let you in when I'm ready?"

Shukhov imagined that he saw Senka's head right in front of the porch. He felt wildly elated, and using his elbows made an effort to push through to him. But, looking at those backs, he knew that it was beyond his powers. He wouldn't get through.

"Twenty-seventh," the Limper called, "go ahead."

The 27th bounded up and made a dash for the door, and the rest surged up after them. Shukhov, among them, was shoving with all his might. The porch quivered, and the lamp overhead protested shrilly.

"What again, you scum?" the Limper shouted in rage. Down came his cudgel, on a shoulder, on a back, pushing the men off, felling one after another.

Again he cleared the steps.

From below Shukhov saw Pavlo at the Limper's side. It was he who led the team to the mess-hall—Tiurin wouldn't demean himself by joining in the hubbub.

"Form fives, hundred and fourth," Pavlo called from the porch. "Make way for them, friends."

Friends: just see them making way, —— 'em.

"Let me through, you in front. That's my team," Shukhov grunted, shoving against a back.

The man would gladly have done so but others were squeezing him from every side.

The crowd heaved, pushing away so that no one could breathe. To get its skilly. Its lawful skilly.

Shukhov tried something else. He grasped the porch-rail on his left, got his arms round a pillar and heaved himself up. He kicked someone's knee and caught a blow in the ribs; a few oaths, but he was through. He planted a foot on the edge of the porch-floor, close to the top step, and waited. Some of his pals who were already there gave him a hand.

The mess-chief walked to the door and looked back.

"Come on, Limper, send in two more teams."

"One hundred and fourth," shouted the Limper. "Where d'you think *you're* crawling, shit?"

He whammed a man from another team on the back of the neck with his cudgel.

"One hundred and fourth," shouted Pavlo, leading in his men.

"Phew!" gasped Shukhov in the mess-hall. And, without waiting for Pavlo's instructions, he started looking for free trays.

The mess-hall seemed as usual, with clouds of vapour curling in through the door and the men sitting shoulder to shoulder—like seeds in a sunflower. Others pushed their way through the tables, and others were carrying loaded trays. Shukhov had grown used to it all over the years and his sharp eyes had noticed that S 208 had only five bowls on the tray he was carrying. This meant that it was the last tray-load for his team. Otherwise the tray would have been full.

He went up to the man and said in his ear:

"After you with that tray."

"Someone's waiting for it at the hatch. I promised. . . ."

"Let him cool his heels, the lazy lag."

They came to an understanding.

S 208 carried his tray to the table and unloaded the bowls. Shukhov immediately grabbed it. At that moment the man it had been promised to ran up and made to seize it. But he was punier than Shukhov. Shukhov shoved him off with the tray—what the hell are you pulling for?—and flung him against a pillar. Then putting the tray under his arm he trotted off to the service-hatch.

Pavlo was standing in the queue there, worried because there was no empty tray. He was delighted to see Shukhov. He pushed the man ahead of him out of the way: "Why are you standing here? Can't you see I've got a tray?"

Look, there was Gopchik—with another tray.

"They were dithering," he said with a laugh, "and I snatched it."

Gopchik will do well. Give him another three years—he has still to grow up—and he'll become nothing less than a bread-cutter. He's fated for it.

Pavlo told him to hand over the second of the trays to Yermo-layev, a hefty Siberian who was serving a ten-year stretch, like Shukhov, for being caught by the Germans; then sent him to keep an eye on any table where the men might be finishing. Shukhov put his tray down and waited.

"One hundred and fourth," announced Pavlo at the hatch.

In all there were five of these hatches: three for serving regular food, one for zeks on special diet (ulcer victims, and book-keeping personnel, as a favour), and one for the return of dirty dishes (that's where the dish-lickers foregathered, sparring with one another). The hatches were low—about waist-level. The cooks themselves were out of sight, only their hands, and the ladles, could be seen.

The cook's hands were white and well cared for, but huge and hairy: a boxer's hands, not a cook's. He took a pencil and made a note on the wall—he kept his list there.

"One hundred and fourth—twenty-four portions."

Panteleyev slopped into the mess-hall. Nothing wrong with him, the son of a bitch.

The cook took an enormous ladle and stirred, stirred, stirred. The cauldron had just been refilled, almost up to the brim, and steam poured from it. Replacing the huge ladle with a smaller one he began serving the skilly. He didn't go deep.

"One, two, three, four. . . ."

Some of the bowls had been filled while the stuff from the bottom of the cauldron hadn't settled yet after the stirring, and some were duds—nothing but liquid. Shukhov made a mental note of which was which. He put ten bowls on his tray and carried them off. Gopchik waved from the second row of pillars.

"Over here, Ivan Denisovich, over here."

No playing the fool with bowls of skilly. Shukhov was careful not to jolt. He kept his throat busy too.

"Hey you, H 920. Gently, uncle. Out of the way, my lad."

It was hard enough, in a crowd like this, to carry a single bowl without slopping it. He was carrying ten. All the same, he put the tray down safely, on the end of the table that Gopchik had cleared. No splashes. He managed, too, so to manoeuvre the tray that the two bowls with the thickest skilly came just opposite the place he was about to sit down in.

Yermolayev brought another ten bowls. Gopchik ran off and came back with Pavlo, the last four in their hands.

Kilgas brought the bread tray. Tonight they were being fed in accordance with the work they had done. Some got 200 grams, some 300, and Shukhov 400. He took a piece with a crust for himself, and 200 grams from the middle of the loaf for Tsezar.

Now from all over the mess-hall Shukhov's team-mates began streaming up, to collect their supper and eat it where they could. As he handed out the bowls, there were two things he had to take care of: he had to remember whom he'd served, and he had to watch out for the tray—and for his own corner of it. (He put his spoon into a bowl—one of the "thick" ones. Reserved, that meant.) Fetiukov was among the first to arrive. But he soon walked off, reckoning there was nothing to be scrounged that particular evening: so better to wander round the mess, scrounging for left-overs (if someone doesn't finish his skilly and pushes his bowl back, there are always people hustling to pounce on it, like vultures).

Shukhov counted the portions with Pavlo. Correct, apparently. He pushed across a bowl for Tiurin, one of the "thick" ones: and Pavlo poured his skilly into a narrow German mess-tin, with a lid —you could carry it under your coat, close to your chest.

The empty trays were handed in. Pavlo sat there with his double helping. Shukhov with his two bowls. And now they had nothing more to say to one another—the sacred moments had come.

Shukhov took off his hat and laid it on his knees. He tasted one bowl, he tasted the other. Not bad, there was some fish in it. Generally, the evening skilly was much thinner than at breakfast: if they're to work, prisoners must be fed in the morning; in the evening they'll go to sleep anyway.

He set to. First he only drank the liquid, drank and drank. As it went down, filling his whole body with warmth, all his guts began to flutter inside him at their meeting with that skilly. Goo-ood! There it comes, that brief moment for which a zek lives.

And now Shukhov complained about nothing: neither about

the length of his stretch, nor about the length of the day, nor about their filching another Sunday. This was all he thought about now: we'll survive. We'll stick it out, God grant, till it's over.

He drained the hot soup from both bowls, and then tipped what was left in the second into the first, scraping it clean with his spoon. That set his mind at ease. Now he didn't have to think about the second and keep an eye or a hand on it.

Now that he could look freely he glanced at his neighbours' bowls. The one on his left was little more than water. The dirty snakes. The tricks they play! And on their fellow-zeks.

He began to eat the cabbage with what was left of the soup. A potato had found its way into one of the bowls—Tsezar's. A medium-sized spud, frost-bitten, hard and sweetish. There wasn't much fish, just a few stray bits of bare backbone. But you must chew every bone, every fin, to suck the juice out of them, for the juice is healthy. It takes time, of course, but he was in no hurry to go anywhere. Today was a red-letter day for him: two helpings for dinner, two helpings for supper. Everything else could wait.

Except, maybe, that visit to the Lett for tobacco. None might be left in the morning.

He supped without bread. A double helping *and* bread—that was going too far. The bread would do for tomorrow. The belly is a rascal. It doesn't remember how well you treated it yesterday, it'll cry out for more tomorrow.

He ate up his skilly without taking much interest in what was happening round him. No need for that: he wasn't on the scrounge for extras, he was eating his own lawful portion. All the same, he noticed that when the fellow opposite got up a tall old man—U 81—sat down in his place. Shukhov knew he was in the 64th and had heard, while waiting in the parcels queue, that the 64th had been sent to the Socialist Way of Life settlement that day instead of the 104th, and had spent the whole time without a chance of getting warm—putting up barbed wire, building their own zone.

He'd been told that this old man had spent years without number in camps and prisons, and that he hadn't benefited from a single amnesty. Whenever one ten-year stretch had run out they shoved another on to him right away.

Now Shukhov looked closely at the man. He held himself straight—the other zeks sat all hunched up—and looked as if he'd put something extra on the bench to sit on. There was nothing left to crop on his head: his hair had dropped out long since—the result of high living, no doubt. His eyes didn't dart after everything going on in the mess-hall. He kept them fixed in an unseeing gaze at some spot over Shukhov's head. His worn wooden spoon dipped rhythmically into the thin skilly, but instead of lowering his head to the bowl like everybody else, he raised the spoon high to his lips. He'd lost all his teeth and chewed his bread with iron gums. All life had drained out of his face but it had been left, not sickly or feeble, but hard and dark like carved stone. And by his hands, big and cracked and blackened, you could see that he'd had little opportunity of doing cushy jobs. But he wasn't going to give in, oh no! *He* wasn't going to put his 300 grams on the dirty, bespattered table—he put it on a well-washed bit of rag.

However, he couldn't go on watching the old man—he had other things to do. He finished his supper, licked his spoon clean and put it in his boot. He pulled his hat over his eyes, got up, picked up his bread and Tsezar's, and went out. Another porch led from the mess-hall. Two more orderlies stood there: they had nothing to do except unhook the door, let people through, and slip the hook on again.

Shukhov came out with a full belly. He felt pleased with himself and decided that, although it was close on time for the "all inside", he'd run over to the Lett all the same. Instead of taking the bread to his hut he strode to Hut 7.

The moon was high—clean and white, as if chiselled out of the sky. It was clear up there and there were some stars out—the brightest of them. But he had even less time for star-gazing than for watching people in the mess-hall. One thing he realized—the frost was no milder. One of the civilians had said, and this had been passed on, that it was likely to drop to −30° in the night, and as low as −40° towards morning.

From far away in the settlement he heard the drone of a tractor. From the direction of the main thoroughfare an excavator squealed shrilly. And creak, creak, went every pair of boots in which people walked or ran about the camp.

There was no wind.

He meant to buy the tobacco at the price he'd paid before—one rouble a glassful, though, outside, that amount would cost three times as much, and for some cuts even more. In forced labour camps all prices were local; it was quite different from anywhere else, because you couldn't save money and few had any at all, for it was very hard to come by. No one was paid a copeck for his work (at Ust-Izhma he'd received at least thirty roubles a month). If anyone's relatives sent money by post he didn't get it in cash anyway, it was credited to his personal account. You could draw on a personal account once a month at the camp-shop to buy soap, mouldy biscuits and "Prima" cigarettes. Whether you liked the wares or not, you had to spend the amount the chief had given you a chit for. If you didn't, the money was lost—written off, if you please.

Shukhov did private jobs to get money, making slippers out of customers' rags—two roubles a pair—or patching torn jackets, price by agreement.

Hut 7, unlike Hut 9, wasn't in two big halves. It had a long passage, with ten doors opening off it. Each room housed a team, packed into seven tiers of bunks. In addition, there was a little cubby-hole for the bucket and another for the senior orderly. The artists had a cubby-hole to themselves, too.

Shukhov headed for the Lett's room. He found him lying on a lower bunk, his feet propped on a ledge. He was talking to his neighbour in Latvian.

Shukhov sat down beside him. "'Evening." "'Evening," replied the Lett, without lowering his feet. The room was small, everyone was listening. Who was he? What did he want?

Both Shukhov and the Lett realized that people were curious, so Shukhov let the conversation drag on. Well, how are you doing? Oh, not so bad. Cold today. Yes.

Shukhov waited until everyone had started talking again (they were arguing about the Korean war: now that the Chinese had joined in, would that mean a world war or not?). He leaned closer to the Lett.

"Any 'baccy?"

"Yes."

"Let's see it."

The Lett dropped his feet off the ledge, put them on the floor, sat up. He was a mean fellow, that Lett—filled a glass with tobacco as if he was afraid of putting in a single pinch too many.

He showed Shukhov his tobacco-pouch and slid open the fastener.

Shukhov took a pinch and laid the shag on his palm. He examined it. Same as last time, brownish, same rough cut. He held it to his nose and sniffed. That was the stuff. But to the Lett he said:

"Not the same, somehow."

"The same, the same," the Lett said testily. "I never have any other kind. Always the same."

"All right," said Shukhov. "Stuff some into a glass for me. I'll have a smoke and perhaps take a second glassful."

He said "stuff" on purpose, because the Lett had the habit of dropping the tobacco in loosely.

The Lett brought out another pouch from under his pillow, fuller than the first. He took his glass out of a locker. It was really a plastic container, but Shukhov reckoned it held the same as an ordinary glass.

The Lett began to fray out the tobacco into the glass.

"Press it down, press it down," said Shukhov, laying his own thumb on it.

"I know how to do it," the Lett said sharply, jerking away the glass and pressing the tobacco, though lightly. He dropped in a little more.

Meanwhile, Shukhov had unbuttoned his jacket and was groping inside the cotton lining for a piece of paper that only he knew where to find. Using both hands he squeezed it through the cotton and forced it along to a little hole in the cloth somewhere quite different, a small tear that he'd tacked with a couple of loose stitches. When the paper reached the hole he snapped the thread with a finger-nail, folded the paper lengthwise (it had already been folded in a longish rectangle), and pulled it through the hole. Two roubles. Worn notes that didn't rustle.

In the room a prisoner shouted:

"D'you mean to say you think Old Whiskers[1] will take pity

[1] Stalin.

108

on you? Why, he wouldn't trust his own brother. You haven't a chance, you weed."

One good thing about these "special" camps: you were free to let off steam. At Ust-Izhma you need only whisper that there was a shortage of matches outside, and they'd put you in the lock-up and add another ten years to your stretch. But here you could bawl anything you liked from the top tier of bunks—the squealers didn't pass it on, the security boys had stopped caring.

The trouble was, you didn't have much time to talk in.

"Ekh, you're making it lie too loose," Shukhov complained.

"Oh well, there you are," said the Lett, adding a pinch on top.

Shukhov took his pouch out of an inside pocket and poured in the tobacco from the glass.

"All right," he said, deciding not to waste the first precious cigarette by smoking it hurriedly. "Stuff it full again."

Wrangling a bit more, he poured the second glassful into his pouch, handed over the two roubles, and left with a nod.

As soon as he was outside again he doubled back to Hut 9. He didn't want to miss Tsezar when he came back with that parcel.

But Tsezar was already there, sitting on his bunk and gloating over the parcel. Its contents were laid out on his bunk and on top of the locker, but as there was no direct light there—Shukhov's bunk was in the way—it wasn't very easy to see.

Shukhov stooped, passed between Tsezar's bunk and the captain's, and handed Tsezar his bread ration.

"Your bread, Tsezar Markovich."

He didn't say "Well, did you get it?" That would have been to hint "I kept that place in the queue and now have a right to my share". The right was his, that he knew, but even eight years as a convict hadn't turned him into a jackal—and the longer he spent at the camp the stronger he made himself.

But his eyes were another matter. Those eyes, the hawk-like eyes of a zek, darted to one side and slid swiftly over what was laid out there; and although the food hadn't been unpacked and some of the bags were still unopened, that quick look and the evidence of his nose told him that Tsezar had got sausage, condensed milk, a plump smoked fish, pork-fat, rusks, biscuits, two kilograms of lump sugar and what looked like butter, as well as cigarettes and pipe tobacco—and that wasn't all.

He learned all this during the brief moment it took him to say: "Your bread, Tsezar Markovich."

Tsezar, all excited and looking a bit tipsy (and who wouldn't, after getting a parcel like that!) waved the bread away:

"Keep it, Ivan Denisovich."

His bowl of skilly, and now this two hundred grams of bread—that was a full supper, and of course Shukhov's fair share of the parcel.

And he put out of his mind any idea of getting something tasty from what Tsezar had laid out. There's nothing worse than working your belly to no purpose.

Well, he had his four hundred grams and now this extra two hundred, besides the piece in his mattress, at least another two hundred grams. Not bad. He'd eat two hundred now and some more later, and still have next day's ration for work. Living high, eh! As for the hunk in the mattress, let it stay there! A good thing he'd found time to sew it in! Someone in the 75th had had a hunk pinched from his locker. That was a dead loss, nothing could be done about it.

People imagine that the parcel a man gets is a sort of nice, tight sack he has only to slit open and be happy. But if you work it out it's a matter of easy come, easy go. Shukhov had known cases when before his parcel arrived a fellow would be doing odd jobs to earn a bit of extra kasha, or cadging fag-ends—just like anybody else. He has to share with the guard and the team-leader—and how can he help giving a little something to the trusty in the parcels-office? Why, next time the fellow may mislay your parcel and a week may go by before your name appears again on the list! And that other fellow at the place where you hand in your food to be kept for you, safe from friskers and pilferers—Tsezar will be there before the morning muster, with everything in a sack—he must have his cut too, and a good one, if you don't want him filching little by little more than you gave him. Sitting there all day, the rat, shut up with other people's food—try to keep an eye on him! And there must be something for services like Shukhov's. And something to the bath attendant for issuing you with decent underwear—not much but something. And for the barber who shaves you "with paper" (for wiping the razor on—he usually does it on your knee). Not much to him either but, still, three or four fags. And at the C.E.D., for your letters to be kept separate and not get lost. And if you want to fiddle a day or two and lie in bed, instead of going to work, you have to slip the doctor a trifle. And what about the neighbour you share a locker with (the captain, in Tsezar's case)? He must have his whack. He sees, after all, every blessed bit you take. Who could be so brazen as not to give him his share?

So leave envy to those who always think the radish in the other fellow's hand is bigger than yours. Shukhov knows life and never opens his belly to what doesn't belong to him.

Meanwhile he pulled off his boots, climbed up to his bunk, took the strip of hacksaw out of his mitten and decided that to-morrow he'd look about for a good pebble and start whetting down the blade to make a cobbling-knife. Four days' work, he reckoned, if he sat over it mornings and evenings, and he'd have a fine little knife with a sharp, curved blade.

But now he had to conceal that find of his, if only till morning. He'd slip it into the edge of the partition under the cross-beam. And as the captain hadn't returned yet to his bunk down below and the sawdust wouldn't fall on his face, Shukhov turned back the head of his mattress and set about hiding the thing.

His top-bunk neighbours could see what he was doing: Alyosha and—across the aisle, in the next tier—the two Estonians. But he didn't worry about them.

Fetiukov walked through the hut. He was sobbing, all hunched up, his mouth smeared with blood. So he'd been beaten up again —the bowls! With no attempt to hide his tears, and looking at no one, he passed the whole team, crawled into his bunk and buried his face in his mattress.

When you thought about it, you couldn't help feeling sorry for him. He wouldn't live to see the end of his stretch. His attitude was all wrong.

Just then the captain turned up. He looked cheerful as he carried a pot of tea, special tea, you bet! Two tea-barrels stood in the hut, but what sort of tea could you call it? Muck: warm water with a touch of colouring, dish-wash smelling of the barrel —of steamed wood and rot. That was tea for the proles. But the captain must have taken a pinch of real tea from Tsezar, put it in his pot and hurried to the hot-water tap. And now, well satisfied, he settled down beside his locker.

"All but scalded my fingers at the tap," he boasted. Down there Tsezar spread a sheet of paper, and began laying this and that on it. Shukhov turned the head of his mattress back. He didn't want to see what was going on; he didn't want to upset himself. But even now they couldn't get along without him: Tsezar rose to his full height, his eyes level with Shukhov's, and winked.

"Ivan Denisovich! Er . . . lend me your 'ten days'."

That meant a small pen-knife. Yes, Shukhov had one: he kept it concealed in the partition. A bit shorter than half a finger but, the little rascal, it cut pork-fat five fingers thick. He'd made the blade himself, mounted it and whetted it sharp.

He crawled to the beam. He fished the knife out. He handed it over. Tsezar nodded and ducked below.

That knife's a bread-winner too. After all, you can be put in the cells for keeping it, and only a man without conscience could say: lend us your knife, we're going to slice some sausage, and you can —— off.

Now Tsezar was again in his debt.

Having settled the bread and knife business, Shukhov opened his tobacco-pouch. First he took a pinch of tobacco out of it, equal to what he'd borrowed, and stretched a hand across the aisle to Eino the Estonian. Thanks.

The Estonian's lips stretched in a sort of smile. He muttered something to his "brother", and together they rolled the pinch of 'baccy into a cigarette. Let's try Shukhov's tobacco.

No worse than yours. Try it, if you please. He'd like to try it himself, but some time-keeper in his brain told him that the evening count would very soon be starting. This was just the time the guards poked round the huts. If he was going to smoke now he'd have to go into the corridor, but up there in his bunk he somehow felt warmer. The hut was as a matter of fact far from warm—that film of frost was still on the ceiling. He'd shiver in the night, but now it was bearable.

Shukhov stayed in his bunk and began crumbling little bits off his bread. He listened unwillingly to Tsezar and Buinovsky, talking below over their tea.

"Help yourself, captain. Help yourself, don't hesitate. Take some of this smoked fish. Have a slice of sausage."

"Thanks, I will."

"Spread some butter on that bread. It's real Moscow bread."

"D'you know, I simply can't believe they're still baking pure white bread anywhere. Such abundance reminds me of a time when I happened to be in Arkhangelsk. . . ."

The two hundred voices in Shukhov's half of the hut were making a terrific din, but he fancied he heard the rail being struck. No one else seemed to have heard it. He also noted that 'Snubnose', the guard, had come into the hut. He was no more than a lad, small and rosy-cheeked. He was holding a sheet of paper, and it was clear from this and his manner that he'd come, not to turn them all out for the evening count or nab smokers, but to get someone.

'Snubnose' checked something on his list and said:

"Where's the hundred and fourth?"

"Here," they answered. The Estonians hid their cigarettes and waved away the smoke.

"Where's the team-leader?"

"Well?" said Tiurin from his bunk, lowering his feet reluctantly.

"Your people written those chits—about the extra stuff they were wearing?"

"They'll write them," said Tiurin with assurance.

"They're overdue."

"My men haven't had much schooling. It's not an easy job. (This about Tsezar and the captain! Good for you, team-leader, you're never at a loss for an answer.) No pens. No ink."

"Ought to have them."

"They take 'em off us."

"Well, look out, team-leader. If you go on talking like that I'll put you in the lock-up with the rest," 'Snubnose' promised Tiurin, but mildly. "Now about those chits—see they're handed in to the guard-room before muster tomorrow morning. And give orders that all prohibited garments are to be surrendered at the clothes-store. Get that?"

"I get it."

(The captain was in luck, thought Shukhov. He hadn't heard a word, he was having such a fine time with his sausage.)

"Let's see now," said the guard. "S 311. He one of yours?"

"Have to look at my list," said Tiurin vaguely. "Expect me to keep all those damned numbers in my head?"

He was playing for time. He wanted to save Buinovsky one night at least, by dragging things out till the count.

"Buinovsky. He here?"

"Eh? Here I am," called the captain from his haven under Shukhov's bunk.

There you are, the quickest louse is always the first to be caught in the comb.

"You? Yes, that's right. S. 311. Get ready."

"Where am I to go?"

"You know where."

The captain sighed. He grunted. Nothing more. It must have been easier for him to take out a squadron of destroyers into the dark, stormy night than to tear himself away from this friendly chat and set out for the icy cells.

"How many days?" he asked, his voice falling.

"Ten. Come on, come on. Get a move on."

At that moment the hut-orderlies shouted:

"Evening count. All out for evening count."

This meant that the guard who was to count them had already entered the hut.

The captain looked round. Should he take his coat? Anyway, they'd strip it off him when he got there, leaving him only his jacket. Better go as he was. He'd hoped that Volkovoi would forget (but Volkovoi never forgot anyone) and had made no preparations, hadn't even hidden a pinch of tobacco in his jacket. And to carry it in his hands—that would be useless, they'd take it from him straight away when they frisked him.

All the same . . . Tsezar slipped him a couple of cigarettes as he put on his hat.

"Well, brothers, goodbye," said the captain with an embarrassed nod to his team-mates, and followed the guard out.

A few voices shouted: Keep your pecker up. But what could you really say to him? They knew the cells, the 104th did, they'd built them. Brick walls, cement floor, no windows, a stove they lit only to melt the ice on the walls and make pools on the floor. You slept on bare boards, and if you'd any teeth left to eat with after all the chattering they'd be doing, they gave you three hundred grams of bread day after day and hot skilly only on the third, sixth and ninth.

Ten days. Ten days "hard" in the cells—if you sat them out to the end your health would be ruined for the rest of your life. T.B. and nothing but hospital for you till you croaked.

As for those who got fifteen days "hard" and sat them out— they went straight into a hole in the cold earth.

As long as you're in a hut—praise the Lord and sit tight.

"Come on now, out you get, before I count three," shouted the hut-commander, "anyone who isn't out will have his number taken. I'll give it to the citizen guard."

The hut-commander was another of the very biggest bastards. After all, just think, he's locked in with us all night, but the airs he puts on, not afraid of anyone! On the contrary, everyone's afraid of him. Some of us he betrays to the guards, others he clouts himself. He lost a thumb in a scrap and is classed as an invalid, but his face is the face of a thug. Actually he *is* a thug with a criminal record, but among the charges against him was one under Article 58, 14, and that's how he landed up with us.

He wouldn't think twice about taking your number and passing it to the guard—and that means two days in the lock-up, with work. So instead of just trailing to the door one by one they all rushed out in a crowd, tumbling down from the bunks as if they were bears and pressing to the narrow exit.

Shukhov, the cigarette in his palm—he'd craved for it so long and had already rolled it—sprang nimbly down, and slipped his feet into his valenki. He was on the point of leaving when he felt a twinge of pity for Tsezar. It wasn't that he wanted to make anything more out of the man, he felt genuinely sorry for him. For all his high opinion of himself, Tsezar didn't know a thing about life: after collecting his parcel he shouldn't have gloated over it, he should have taken it to the store-room right away before the evening count. Eating's something that can wait. But now what was Tsezar going to do with all that stuff? He couldn't carry his sack with him to the count. What a horse-laugh that would mean! Four hundred zeks roaring their heads off. But to leave it in the hut no matter how briefly meant that the first to run back from the count would pinch it. (At Ust-Izhma it was even crueller:

there, when we came back from work, the criminals got ahead and cleaned out all our lockers.)

Shukhov saw that Tsezar realized the danger. He was bustling here and there, but too late. He was stuffing the sausage and pork-fat under his jacket. That at least he could save by taking it to the count.

Pityingly, Shukhov gave him some advice:

"Sit here till the last moment, Tsezar Markovich. Hide here in the shadow and stay till everyone has left. And when the guard comes round the bunks with the orderlies and looks into all the nooks and crannies, come out and say you're feeling bad. I'll go out first and I'll be back first. That's the way. . . ."

And he ran off.

At first he elbowed his way through the crowd mercilessly (protecting his cigarette in his fist, however). In the corridor, which served both halves of the hut, and near the door, the men in front were hanging back, the wily beasts, clinging in two rows to the walls on each side, leaving just enough room for any fool who liked the cold to squeeze through. They were going to stay here, they've been out all day. Why should they freeze needlessly for another ten minutes? No fools here! You croak today but *I* mean to live till tomorrow.

At any other time Shukhov too would have clung to the wall. But now he strode to the door and even grinned:

"What are you scared of, you ninnies? Never seen Siberian frost before? Come outside and warm yourselves by the wolf's sun. Give us a light, uncle."

He lit his cigarette at the door and moved out on to the porch. "Wolf's sun", that's what they'd called the moon in Shukhov's village.

The moon rode high now. As high again, and it would be at its zenith. The sky was greenish-white, the rare stars shone brilliantly. The snow gleamed white, the barrack walls gleamed white. The lamps had little effect.

There was a dense black cloud outside one of the huts. The zeks had come out for the count. They were coming out over there too. But it wasn't the sound of voices you heard from the barracks—it was the creaking of boots on the snow.

Some prisoners were coming down the steps and forming up,

opposite the hut. Five in front, then three behind. Shukhov joined the three. After an extra bit of bread, and with a cigarette between your lips, it wasn't so bad standing there. Good tobacco—the Lett hadn't done him in. Strong, and smelled good.

Gradually, other prisoners trailed through the door. Two or three more lines of five were forming behind him. They came out angry now. Why were those rats jostling in the corridor? Why weren't they coming out? Why should we have to freeze for them?

No zek ever saw a clock or a watch. What use were they to him anyway? All he needs to know is: will reveille sound soon? How long to the muster? How long to dinner? To the last clanging of the rail?

The evening count, everyone said, was at nine. But it never finished at nine—they would sometimes recount twice, and then even again. You never got away before ten. And at five o'clock next morning they hounded you out of your bunk with the first clanging of the rail. No wonder that Moldavian had kipped down at the shop before work was over today. Wherever a zek gets a bit of warmth into him he falls asleep on the spot. You lose so much sleep during the week that on Sunday—provided they don't send you to work—whole hutfuls of zeks sleep the day through.

Now they're streaming forward. At last! The hut-commander and the guard were slinging them out, kicking their arses. Serve 'em right, the sly beasts.

"What?" the zeks in front shouted at the late-comers. "Being clever, eh? Want to lick the cream of the shit, you rats? If you'd come out earlier we'd be through now."

The whole hut had been emptied. Four hundred men—eighty ranks of five. They formed up in a column, the ones in front strictly in fives, the others any old how.

"Get into line there, you at the back," the hut-commander shouted from the steps.

They didn't move, —— 'em.

Tsezar came out shivering, shamming illness. At his heels were four orderlies, two from each half of the hut, and a prisoner who limped. They stood in front so that Shukhov was now a row further back. Tsezar was sent to the rear of the column.

The guard came out too.

"Form fives!" he shouted to the rear of the column, furiously.

"Form fives" shouted the hut-commander even more furiously. The men didn't budge, —— 'em.

The hut-commander rushed from the porch to the rear of the column, swearing and hitting out.

But he was careful whom he hit. Only the meek ones.

The ranks formed up. He came back. He shouted:

"First. Second. Third. . . ."

Directly they'd been counted the men broke away and rushed into the hut. All square for today with the authorities.

All square, unless there's a recount. Those parasites were such dolts, they counted worse than any herdsman. For all that he may be unable to read or write, a herdsman knows if there's a calf missing when he's driving the herd. And these parasites had been trained, much good it'd done them.

The previous winter there'd been no drying sheds at all for the boots, and the zeks had had to leave their valenki in the huts night after night. So if the count was repeated, everyone had to be driven outside again, a second, a third, a fourth time—already undressed, just as they were, wrapped in blankets. Since then a drying shed had been built; it wasn't big enough for all the boots at one time, but at least each of the teams could get the benefit of it once every two or three days. So now any recount was held inside. They merely shifted the zeks from one half of the hut to the other, counting them as they filed through.

Shukhov wasn't the first to be back, but he kept an eye on anyone ahead of him. He ran up to Tsezar's bunk and sat on it. He took off his boots, and climbed on to the upper tier of a frame of bunks close by the stove. He put his boots on the stove—first-comer's prerogative—then back to Tsezar's bunk. He sat there cross-legged, one eye on guard for Tsezar (they might snitch his packages from under the head of his bunk), the other for himself (they might push his boots off the stove).

"Hey," he shouted, "hey you, Ginger. Want to feel that boot in your teeth? Put your own up but don't touch other peoples' ".

The prisoners poured in like a stream.

The lads in the 20th shouted:

"Give us your boots."

Directly they'd left the hut with the boots the door was locked after them. When they ran back they shouted:

"Citizen chief. Let us in."

And the guards gathered in their quarters with their boards and did the book-keeping: had anyone bolted, or was everything in order?

Well, Shukhov needn't think about such things that evening. Here came Tsezar, diving between the tiers of bunks on his way back.

"Thank you, Ivan Denisovich."

Shukhov nodded, and shot up into his bunk like a squirrel. Now he could finish his bread, smoke a second cigarette, go to sleep.

But he'd had such a good day, he felt in such good spirits, that somehow he wasn't in the mood for sleep yet.

He must make his bed now—there wasn't much to it. Strip his mattress of the grubby blanket and lie on it (it must have been '41 when he last slept in sheets—that was at home; it even seemed odd for women to bother about sheets, all that extra laundering). Head on the pillow, stuffed with shavings of wood: feet in jacket sleeve; coat on top of blanket and—Glory be to thee, O Lord. Another day over. Thank You I'm not spending tonight in the cells. Here it's still bearable.

He lay head to the window, but Alyosha, who slept next to him on the same level, across a low wooden railing, lay the opposite way, to catch the light. He was reading his Bible again.

The electric light was quite near. You could read and even sew by it.

Alyosha heard Shukhov's whispered prayer, and, turning to him:

"There you are, Ivan Denisovich, your soul is begging to pray. Why, then, don't you give it its freedom?"

Shukhov stole a look at him. Alyosha's eyes glowed like two candles.

"Well, Alyosha," he said with a sigh, "it's this way. Prayers are like those appeals of ours. Either they don't get through or they're returned with 'rejected' scrawled across 'em."

Outside the staff-hut were four sealed boxes—they were cleared by a security officer once a month. Many were the appeals that were dropped into them. The writers waited, counting the weeks: there'll be a reply in two months, in one month. . . .

But the reply doesn't come. Or if it does it's only "rejected".

"But, Ivan Denisovich, it's because you pray too rarely, and badly at that. Without really trying. That's why your prayers stay unanswered. One must never stop praying. If you have real faith you tell a mountain to move and it will move. . . ."

Shukhov grinned and rolled another cigarette. He took a light from the Estonian.

"Don't talk bunkum, Alyosha. I've never seen a mountain move. Well, to tell the truth, I've never seen a mountain at all. But you, now, you prayed in the Caucasus with all that Baptist club of yours—did you make a single mountain move?"

They were a luckless lot too. What harm did they do anyone by praying to God? Every man Jack of 'em given twenty-five years. Nowadays they cut all cloth to the same measure—twenty-five years.

"Oh, we didn't pray for that, Ivan Denisovich," Alyosha said earnestly. Bible in hand, he drew nearer to Shukhov till they lay face to face. "Of all earthly and mortal things Our Lord commanded us to pray only for our daily bread. 'Give us this day our daily bread.' "

"Our ration, you mean?" asked Shukhov.

But Alyosha didn't give up. Arguing more with his eyes than his tongue, he plucked at Shukhov's sleeve, stroked his arm, and said:

"Ivan Denisovich, you shouldn't pray to get parcels or for extra skilly, not for that. Things that man puts a high price on are vile in the eyes of Our Lord. We must pray about things of the spirit—that the Lord Jesus should remove the scum of anger from our hearts. . . ."

"Listen to me. At our church in Polomnya we had a priest . . ."

"Don't talk to me about your priest," Alyosha said imploringly, his brow furrowed with distress.

"No, listen." Shukhov propped himself up on an elbow. "In Polomnya, our parish, there isn't a man richer than the priest. Take roofing, for instance. We charge thirty-five roubles a day to ordinary folk for mending a roof, but the priest a hundred. And he forks up without a murmur. He pays alimony to three women in three different towns, and he's living with a fourth. And he keeps that bishop of his on a hook, I can tell you. Oh yes, he gives his fat hand to the bishop, our priest does. And he's ousted every other priest they've sent there. Wouldn't share a thing with 'em."

"Why are you talking to me about priests? The Orthodox Church has departed from Scripture. It's because their faith is unstable that they're not in prison."

Shukhov went on calmly smoking and watching his excited companion.

"Alyosha," he said, withdrawing his arm and blowing smoke into his face. "I'm not against God, understand that. I readily believe in God. But I don't believe in paradise or in hell. Why d'you take us for fools and stuff us with your paradise and hell stories? That's what I don't like."

He lay back, dropping his cigarette-ash with care between the bunk-frame and the window, so as to singe nothing of the captain's below. He sank into his own thoughts. He didn't hear Alyosha's mumbling.

"Well," he said conclusively, "however much you pray it doesn't shorten your stretch. You'll sit it out from beginning to end anyhow."

"Oh, you mustn't pray for that either," said Alyosha, horrified. "Why d'you want freedom? In freedom your last grain of faith will be choked with weeds. You should rejoice that you're in prison. Here you have time to think about your soul. As the Apostle Paul wrote: 'Why all these tears? Why are you trying to weaken my resolution? For my part I am ready not merely to be bound but even to die for the name of Lord Jesus.' "

Shukov gazed at the ceiling in silence. Now he didn't know either whether he wanted freedom or not. At first he'd longed for it. Every night he'd counted the days of his stretch—how many had passed, how many were coming. And then he'd grown bored with counting. And then it became clear that men of his like wouldn't ever be allowed to return home, that they'd be exiled. And whether his life would be any better there than here—who could tell?

Freedom meant one thing to him—home.

But they wouldn't let him go home.

Alyosha was speaking the truth. His voice and his eyes left no doubt that he was happy in prison.

"You see, Alyosha," Shukov explained to him, "somehow it

works out all right for you: Jesus Christ wanted you to sit in prison and so you are—sitting there for His sake. But for whose sake am *I* here? Because we weren't ready for war in 'forty-one? For that? But was that *my* fault?"

"Seems there's not going to be a recount," Kilgas murmured from his bunk.

"Aye," said Shukhov. "We ought to write it up in coal inside the chimney. No second count." He yawned. "Might as well be off to sleep."

And at that very moment the door-bolt rattled to break the calm that now reigned in the hut. From the corridor ran two of the prisoners who'd taken boots to the drying shed.

"Second count," they shouted.

On their heels came a guard.

"All out to the other half."

Some were already asleep. They began to grumble and shift about, they put their boots on (no one ever took his wadded trousers off at night—you'd grow numb with cold unless you wore them under your blanket).

"Damn them," said Shukhov. Mildly, because he hadn't gone to sleep yet.

Tsezar raised a hand and gave him two biscuits, two lumps of sugar and a slice of sausage.

"Thank you, Tsezar Markovich," said Shukhov, leaning over the edge of his bunk. "Come on, now, hand me over that sack of yours to put under my mattress." (You can't so easily filch things from the bunks on top as you go by. Anyway, who'd look for anything in Shukhov's bunk?)

Tsezar handed up his sack and Shukov hid it under the mattress. Then he waited a little till more men had been sent out—he wouldn't have to stand barefoot so long in the corridor. But the guard scowled at him and shouted:

"Come on, you there in the corner."

Shukhov sprang lightly to the floor (his boots and foot-cloths were so well placed on the stove it would be a pity to move them). Though he'd made so many slippers for others he hadn't a pair of his own. But he was used to this —and the count didn't take long.

They confiscate slippers too if they find them in daytime.

As for the teams who'd sent their boots to be dried, it wasn't so bad for them, now the recount was held indoors. Some wore slippers, some just their foot-cloths, some went barefoot.

"Come on, come on," growled the guard.

"D'you want helping out, you trash?" the hut-commander shouted.

They shoved them all into the other half of the hut, and laggards into the corridor. Shukhov stood against the wall near the bucket. The floor was wettish underfoot. An icy draught crept in from the porch.

They had them all out now and once again the guard and the orderly did their round, looking for any who might be dozing in dark corners. There'd be trouble if they counted short. It would mean still another recount. Round they went, round they went, and came back to the door.

"One, two, three, four. . . ." Now they released you faster, for they were counting one by one. Shukhov managed to squeeze in eighteenth. He ran back to his bunk, put his foot on the support—a heave, and he was up.

All right. Feet back into the sleeve of his jacket. Blanket on top. Then the coat. And to sleep. Now they'd be letting everybody from the other half of the hut into our half. But that's not our worry.

Tsezar returned. Shukhov lowered his sack to him.

Alyosha returned. Unpractical, that's his trouble. Makes himself nice to everyone but doesn't know how to earn anything.

"Here you are, Alyosha," said Shukhov, and handed him a biscuit.

Alyosha smiled.

"Thank you. But you've nothing yourself."

"Eat it."

(We've nothing but we're always earning.)

Now for that slice of sausage. Into the mouth. Getting your teeth into it. Your teeth. The meaty taste. And the meaty juice, the real stuff. Down it goes, into your belly.

Gone.

The rest, Shukhov decided, for the morning. Before the muster. And he buried his head in the thin, unwashed blanket, deaf

123

now to the crowd of zeks from the other half as they jostled between the bunk-frames, waiting to be counted.

Shukhov went to sleep fully content. He'd had many strokes of luck that day: they hadn't put him in the cells; they hadn't sent the team to the settlement; he'd pinched a bowl of kasha at dinner; the team-leader had fixed the rates well; he'd built a wall and enjoyed doing it; he'd smuggled that bit of hacksaw-blade through; he'd earned something from Tsezar in the evening; he'd bought that tobacco. And he hadn't fallen ill. He'd got over it.

A day without a dark cloud. Almost a happy day.

There were three thousand six hundred and fifty-three days like that in his stretch. From the first clang of the rail to the last clang of the rail.

The three extra days were for leap years.

124

TITLES IN THE NEW WINDMILL SERIES

Chinua Achebe: *Things Fall Apart*
Louisa M. Alcott: *Little Women*
Elizabeth Allen: *Deitz and Denny*
Margery Allingham: *The Tiger in the Smoke*
Michael Anthony: *The Year in San Fernando*
Enid Bagnold: *National Velvet*
Stan Barstow: *Joby*
H. Mortimer Batten: *The Singing Forest*
Nina Bawden: *On the Run; The Witch's Daughter; A Handful of Thieves;
    Carrie's War; Rebel on a Rock*
Rex Benedict: *Last Stand at Goodbye Gulch*
Phyllis Bentley: *The Adventures of Tom Leigh*
Paul Berna: *Flood Warning*
Pierre Boulle: *The Bridge on the River Kwai*
E. R. Braithwaite: *To Sir, With Love*
D. K. Broster: *The Flight of the Heron; The Gleam in the North*
F. Hodgson Burnett: *The Secret Garden*
Helen Bush: *Mary Anning's Treasures*
A. Calder-Marshall: *The Man from Devil's Island*
John Caldwell: *Desperate Voyage*
Albert Camus: *The Outsider*
Victor Canning: *The Runaways; Flight of the Grey Goose*
Erskine Childers: *The Riddle of the Sands*
John Christopher: *The Guardians; The Lotus Caves*
Richard Church: *The Cave; Over the Bridge; The White Doe*
Colette: *My Mother's House*
Alexander Cordell: *The Traitor Within*
Margaret Craven: *I Heard the Owl Call my Name*
Roald Dahl: *Danny, Champion of the World; The Wonderful Story of Henry Sugar*
Meindert deJong: *The Wheel on the School*
Peter Dickinson: *The Gift; Annerton Pit*
Eleanor Doorly: *The Radium Woman; The Microbe Man; The Insect Man*
Gerald Durrell: *Three Singles to Adventure; The Drunken Forest; Encounters with
    Animals*
Elizabeth Enright: *Thimble Summer; The Saturdays*
C. S. Forester: *The General*
Eve Garnett: *The Family from One End Street; Further Adventures of the Family
    from One End Street; Holiday at the Dew Drop Inn*
G. M. Glaskin: *A Waltz through the Hills*
Rumer Godden: *Black Narcissus*
Angus Graham: *The Golden Grindstone*
Graham Greene: *The Third Man* and *The Fallen Idol*
Grey Owl: *Sajo and her Beaver People*
John Griffin: *Skulker Wheat and Other Stories*
G. and W. Grossmith: *The Diary of a Nobody*
René Guillot: *Kpo the Leopard*
Esther Hautzig: *The Endless Steppe*
Jan De Hartog: *The Lost Sea*
Erik Haugaard: *The Little Fishes*
Bessie Head: *When Rain Clouds Gather*
Ernest Hemingway: *The Old Man and the Sea*
John Hersey: *A Single Pebble*
Georgette Heyer: *Regency Buck*

Alfred Hitchcock: *Sinister Spies*
C. Walter Hodges: *The Overland Launch*
Geoffrey Household: *Rogue Male; A Rough Shoot; Prisoner of the Indies; Escape into Daylight*
Fred Hoyle: *The Black Cloud*
Irene Hunt: *Across Five Aprils*
Henry James: *Washington Square*
Josephine Kamm: *Young Mother; Out of Step; Where Do We Go From Here?; The Starting Point*
Erich Kästner: *Emil and the Detectives; Lottie and Lisa*
Clive King: *Me and My Million*
John Knowles: *A Separate Peace*
D. H. Lawrence: *Sea and Sardinia; The Fox* and *The Virgin and the Gipsy; Selected Tales*
Marghanita Laski: *Little Boy Lost*
Harper Lee: *To Kill a Mockingbird*
Laurie Lee: *As I Walked Out One Mid-Summer Morning*
Ursula Le Guin: *A Wizard of Earthsea; The Tombs of Atuan; The Farthest Shore; A Very Long Way from Anywhere Else*
Doris Lessing: *The Grass is Singing*
C. Day Lewis: *The Otterbury Incident*
Lorna Lewis: *Leonardo the Inventor*
Martin Lindsay: *The Epic of Captain Scott*
David Line: *Run for Your Life; Mike and Me*
Kathleen Lines: *The House of the Nightmare; The Haunted and the Haunters*
Joan Lingard: *Across the Barricades; Into Exile; The Clearance*
Penelope Lively: *The Ghost of Thomas Kempe*
Jack London: *The Call of the Wild; White Fang*
Carson McCullers: *The Member of the Wedding*
Lee McGiffen: *On the Trail to Sacramento*
Wolf Mankowitz: *A Kid for Two Farthings*
Olivia Manning: *The Play Room*
Jan Mark: *Thunder and Lightnings*
James Vance Marshall: *A River Ran Out of Eden; Walkabout; My Boy John that Went to Sea*
David Martin: *The Cabby's Daughter*
J. P. Martin: *Uncle*
John Masefield: *The Bird of Dawning; The Midnight Folk; The Box of Delights*
W. Somerset Maugham: *The Kite and Other Stories*
Guy de Maupassant: *Prisoners of War and Other Stories*
Laurence Meynell: *Builder and Dreamer*
Yvonne Mitchell: *Cathy Away*
Honoré Morrow: *The Splendid Journey*
Bill Naughton: *The Goalkeeper's Revenge; A Dog Called Nelson; My Pal Spadger*
E. Nesbit: *The Railway Children; The Story of the Treasure Seekers*
E. Neville: *It's Like this, Cat*
Wilfrid Noyce: *South Col*
Robert C. O'Brien: *Mrs Frisby and the Rats of NIMH; Z for Zachariah*
Scott O'Dell: *Island of the Blue Dolphins*
George Orwell: *Animal Farm*
K. M. Peyton: *Flambards*
Philippa Pearce: *Tom's Midnight Garden*
John Prebble: *The Buffalo Soldiers*